Mrs Freeman Miller

Johnny Nolan was an unwanted boy and by force of circumstances lived the life of an unwanted boy. From one foster home to another he went longing to find a "home" that wanted a "boy" and not a slave, a mischief, or a troublemaker.

Johnny's friends always seemed to be the wrong kind. But he always found some friends, or they always found him. The welfare people and the law, although both were interested in him, couldn't quite keep up with Johnny.

At the last he found a "home" where "foster parents" were like real parents. It was then that Johnny shook his head and said, "I can't believe things are coming out this good for me."

Welfare Kid

BY DAVE HILL

Illustrated by Allan Eitzen

HERALD PRESS,
SCOTTDALE, PENNSYLVANIA

For My Father . . .

Contents

1

I Didn't Steal Nothing

JOHNNY NOLAN was in trouble again.

As soon as he rounded the corner on Sixteenth Avenue and saw the familiar gray coupe with the words *Wentworth Agency* stenciled on the door, he knew it meant trouble for him. And then, when he saw the red pickup in the driveway, which meant that Mr. Benson was home from work early, he knew it was real trouble.

I didn't do anything! But—what difference does that make? As long as they think I've done something, that's all it takes to make trouble. He brushed the blond hair off his forehead as he stood on the sidewalk, schoolbooks under his arm, scuffing his toe on the sidewalk. *Trouble.* He looked up, shrugged, and started walking toward the big clapboard house. The bright May afternoon seemed to have suddenly gone gray and gloomy.

He started around the side of the house, then turned and jumped up on the porch. *Might as well go in the front door. They'll be there anyway, waiting.* He could picture just how they'd look. Mrs. Benson, her long brown hair not quite neat, sitting on a low hassock, chewing her lip and knitting; Mr. Benson, standing in front of the fireplace, puffing on the stub of a cigar and rocking back and forth on his heels; and Miss Parsons, sitting stiffly in a straight-backed chair, her plain black dress buttoned up tightly. She would probably be fiddling with her steel-rimmed glasses.

He grunted as he walked in the door. Everything was exactly as he had known it would be. Then he caught an unexpected face at the far end of the sofa and turned to find himself facing Mr. Conrad, assistant principal of Somerset School. *So that's what the trouble's about! But I never did it!*

Miss Parsons saw him first. "Hello, John," she said, her voice rasping a little more than usual. "We've been talking about you. Come in and sit down."

"Don't track your shoes in here," Mrs. Benson said, not looking up from her knitting. Johnny kicked his shoes off in the hallway and padded across the room, sitting down finally on the floor by the sofa. He chose the end away from Mr. Conrad.

"You have a few things to explain to us," Miss Parsons said. "That's why Mr. Benson called for me today. You *do* know what I'm talking about, don't you, John?" She looked straight at him when she spoke, and Johnny had the odd feeling that she

looked at cabbages in exactly the same way when she went shopping.

"Where'd you get all this junk?" Mr. Benson's voice was harsh and full of anger. Johnny turned to see him pick up a cardboard box and spill the contents out on the coffee table—a tin tray of water colors, pencils, rags, brushes, shading stumps, erasers, sketch pads, and a dozen finished and half-done drawings and water colors.

"I found those in his closet this morning," Mrs. Benson said. She spoke as though Johnny weren't even in the room. "He had them hidden in the closet, under some old quilts."

"I never hid them!" Johnny said. "I—I just put them there."

"Why?"

He shrugged. "I just did. I ain't done nothing!"

"Haven't done anything, John," Miss Parsons said sourly. "Only it appears that you have. And sit up straight and look at people when they talk to you."

"I know what you think," Johnny said. "But I never stole it." He glanced up at Mr. Conrad. "You told them I stole the money, didn't you? I know why you're here! But I didn't do it!"

"Stole what money?" Mr. Conrad asked with a glint in his eyes. "Nobody has accused you of stealing anything—yet. What do you know about money being stolen?"

"All the kids at school know about it," Johnny said. "You know they do too."

"Humph!" Mr. Benson grunted. He rocked back on his heels. "A guilty conscience, that's what. I knew that boy was trouble the day we took him. I told you so, Helen. I just knew it."

Mrs. Benson just nodded and kept knitting. "We still want to know how you paid for those paints and things, Johnny."

"I bought 'em," he said in a low voice.

"We *know* that, John," Miss Parsons said. "At Carpenter's Hobby Shop. I went in to see Mr. Carpenter and he told me you came in and bought them last week—with a ten-dollar bill. Where did you get ten dollars, John?"

10

"I didn't steal it! You think I did, but I never stole nothing!" He looked up at Mr. Conrad. "You think I stole it, don't you? You said I stole it, didn't you? DIDN'T YOU?"

Mr. Conrad cleared his voice. "Well, John, we both know that Miss Nixon had her purse rifled during recess last week—and she is your homeroom teacher. And she *did* have about twelve dollars stolen. And you—well—" He shrugged and spread his hands. "I mean, since you are—"

"I DIDN'T STEAL IT!" Johnny shouted, jumping to his feet. "I never stole anything."

"Where'd you get the money then?" Mr. Benson barked. "Did a little bird bring it to you? You're not a good liar, boy."

"I—I—" Johnny stared wildly at the floor. *What could he say? He knew he hadn't stolen anything, but how could he tell them? He couldn't tell on Dad! He just couldn't tell. He'd promised!* "I—I found it," he said weakly. "On the street."

"John!" Miss Parsons said sharply. "Tell the truth. It won't do you any good to lie now."

"I never stole it!"

Mr. Conrad stood up and dabbed at his forehead with his handkerchief. "Well, I can see that this is a waste of time. He won't admit it, even when he's been caught red-handed, as it were."

"RRRrripp!" Johnny turned to see Mr. Benson ripping a watercolor painting in half. He tried to grab it. "No! You can't! That's mine!"

But Mr. Benson took him firmly by the shoulder and pushed him back down on the sofa. "Steal money—and then waste it on tripe like this." He

11

took up a charcoal sketch and tore it to shreds. "Humph! I knew it was going to mean trouble when we first took you in."

"We've had our share of trouble with him at Somerset, too," Mr. Conrad said. "But then, you can't blame the boy completely. After all, he—"

"DROP DEAD!" Johnny screamed at him. "I HATE YOU! All of you!" He jumped up, tears streaming down his face. Mr. Benson stood stock-still, a half-torn painting in his hands. Everyone stood where they were, frozen into inaction by his outburst.

"Don't tear my pictures up!" he sobbed at Mr. Benson. "If my dad was here, he'd make you quit it. You ain't my dad! I hate you!"

"John!" Miss Parsons said. "I think you had best apologize right now. Mr. Conrad has only said what appears to be the truth."

"I never stole the money! If I had folks like other kids, you'd never pick me out and say I stole the money. Just cause I'm a welfare kid, you think I'm the one who did it!"

"It was a mistake for us to take that boy," Mr. Benson said to no one in particular.

"I hate you! All of you!" Johnny sobbed. "I don't care what you say I never stole it! And I don't care what you do! I don't want to stay here anymore. I hate you!" He broke into choking sobs and ran from the room, up the stairs, and into his room, slamming the door behind him so hard that the windows rattled. He threw himself facedown on the bed and buried his head in his pillow to smother his sobs.

Downstairs he heard the door open and close as Mr. Conrad left. And then he heard the soft conversation of the Bensons and Miss Parsons. He caught snatches of words, enough to tell him what they were saying. He'd heard it all before, too many times. *"Can't handle him anymore . . . he's not happy here . . . we've tried our best . . . find a new home for him . . . maybe a farm . . . with other children his own age . . . my wife's nerves . . . can't put up with his tantrums . . . too much trouble . . . let him go as soon as you find a place . . . ."*

He pulled the pillow tightly around his head to drown out their voices. He didn't care what they did. He'd never liked the Bensons anyway. Mrs. Benson and her knitting, always harping at him, don't do this, don't do that, talk slower, pick up this, put that away, don't slouch, don't run . . . .

And Mr. Benson, grunting and snorting, making fun of him for not playing baseball, laughing at him and calling him a sissy, teasing him for reading so much, making a joke of his drawing, whipping him when he came home crying after losing a fight, talking about his dad. . . .

That hurt the most. *But I never told on you, did I, Dad? I never told!* He could still remember his dad saying, "A man who can't keep his word ain't no kind of man at all." His dad had said that last week when he'd come to meet Johnny after school, and made him promise not to tell anyone.

Johnny knew why. The divorce agreement had said that Dad wasn't supposed to visit him without going through the Wentworth Agency. That had been written right into the divorce. Johnny still remembered how confused he'd been when Miss Parsons had first explained it to him.

But Dad had come to see him anyway, meeting him on the street after school. He'd given Johnny ten dollars, and he'd been drinking again. Dad had acted as if Johnny couldn't tell, but he was almost thirteen, and he knew.

And he knew that if Miss Parsons had found out about it, she might not let Dad see him again till —till she felt like it! That's why he couldn't tell them where he'd *really* gotten the money. Johnny sat up on the bed, almost smiling again. *I didn't tell on you, Dad! Let them think what they will!*

He fingered the chain around his neck. It was a silver chain, with an old-fashioned Canadian penny on it. The penny was sawed in half, and the other half was on a chain Dad wore. He'd given it to Johnny when he saw him in court the day the judge placed him in the agency's care. "As long as you got that, you'll never be broke," Dad had said, grinning. He rubbed the shiny coin in his hand. *I never told on you, Dad!*

A soft tapping at the door announced Mrs. Benson and Johnny turned and frowned at the sound. "Come on in," he mumbled, rubbing his eyes dry. He knew exactly what she was going to say. He'd heard it all before—*Johnny, we've tried our best ... it hasn't worked out ... Miss Parsons is going to find a new home for you ... maybe on a farm ... we're sorry ... we think this is best....*

The door opened and he waited, staring at the quilt. He felt like crying, but he wasn't going to. He hadn't the last time, and he wouldn't now.

14

By Saturday morning it was all settled and arranged. His few belongings were all packed, and they even let him keep his paints. And he *was* going to a farm. "Some fine, older people named Olaffson are going to take you on their farm near Hastings for the summer," Miss Parsons had said. "I hope you do appreciate it, John."

There were still two weeks of school left, but they were going to pass him to the seventh grade anyway. That was all he knew and, when Miss Parsons came to get him Saturday morning, he was on the front porch waiting. Mr. Benson was in the basement and managed to avoid having to say good-bye. Mrs. Benson stood on the front porch waving until they were out of sight, but she didn't look sad at all.

2

You're Not Here for a Vacation!

JOHNNY sat staring out the window of the car, but he didn't really see the green fields and scattered farmhouses they passed. His whole mind was filled with just one idea: *What's this one going to be like?* He counted on his fingers, trying to remember all the foster homes he'd been in. But he found that he couldn't.

First had been the Carlsons. He remembered them because they had been with him at the court hearing when Mom and Dad got their divorce, and Mom had started screaming. And then Mr. Carlson had gotten sick and he'd had to leave. Then had come the Barnes—no, the Barnetts at Clear Lake, on a farm. He remembered that mostly as sunburn and a sore back. He'd been glad when fall came and he moved back to St. Paul for school. The next two he just couldn't remember. But he knew he'd hated both of them.

After that was the Bjorklunds, with the sick old grandfather. He'd had to clean up after him, emptying bedpans while the old man swore at him. And the Winstons and two families named Smith. One of the Smith families he remembered by the smell of cats that filled the house. And then had been the Daltons, where they'd had burned eggs for breakfast every morning. He knew there were at least two more, but he couldn't remember their names, or when he'd lived there. How many would this one make, eleven or twelve? Miss Parsons would know. He asked her.

"This? This is the twelfth home we've had to find for you, John. In less than five years. You've been a real problem for the agency. You had better learn to like this home. They're getting hard to find."

He shrugged and stared at her. She was wearing a black dress again. In all the years she had been his caseworker, three things about her had never changed: she never wore anything but black, she never laughed, and she never called him anything but John. He didn't really know just how he felt about her. He didn't hate her, and he didn't like her. She was just a tall, gray-haired old woman who had become a part of his life, like the weather or something.

"How much farther is it?"

"We're almost there. Are you getting anxious, or are you just glad to be getting away from the Bensons? I shouldn't blame you, after the way you repaid them for their kindness."

17

"I never took that money," Johnny said stubbornly.

"Well, say what you like," she said, shaking her head. "But I can tell you one thing, John. You'll find that Mr. Olaffson won't tolerate a boy who lies. He knows how to break a boy of that habit."

Johnny grunted while she waited for an answer. When none came, she shrugged and drove slowly down the road, rounding a curve, and taking a dirt road down off the highway. She coasted into a farmyard, with a big white house near the road, and across from it a red barn, flanked by a concrete silo and a cluster of gray sheds. A heavy, gray-haired woman in a flour sack apron came out on the porch and waved to them. "That's Mrs. Olaffson now."

"I can see," Johnny answered sullenly.

"Keep a civil tongue, young man! Now get out. There's Mr. Olaffson over by the barn now."

Johnny opened the car door and jumped out. He saw a man walking toward them from the barn. He was tall, with a heavy belly and a long, walrus-like moustache. He looked old, but strong, and he wore a tobacco-stained undershirt under bright red suspenders. He lumbered toward them, chewing away and not smiling.

Mrs. Olaffson talked enough for both of them. "So this is little Johnny," she said, patting him on the head like a chick. "My, but he's thin. Why, he isn't really twelve, is—"

"I'll be thirteen in July," Johnny said, brushing the hair out of his eyes.

"Goodness, but you're thin, child!"

"We'll have to work some muscle on him," Mr.

Olaffson said, walking up and circling Johnny's arm in one big, work-calloused hand. "We'll sweat some meat on your bones, lad." His voice was gravelly and Johnny saw that his eyes were coal black. He smiled stiffly.

"Well, I don't think there's too much to explain," Miss Parsons said. "I suppose he can take his things in the house now, and start getting settled here."

"I'll bet he's hungry," Mrs. Olaffson said. "We'll have to have a little snack."

"I've got a tool shed to finish painting," Mr. Olaffson said. "You give the boy a bit to eat, Olga, and then send him out back. Make sure he puts work clothes on." He turned and lumbered toward the barn without another word.

"Nels is a little abrupt at times," Mrs. Olaffson said hastily. "But I'm sure Johnny will get on well here. Now, let's see about getting his things put away."

An hour later, Johnny wiped up the last of a plate of beans with a sop of bread and picked up his glass. "Can I have a little more milk, please?"

Glancing nervously toward the door, Mrs. Olaffson poured him a half-full glass. "You best drink it quickly, son," she said. "The Mister, he's a hard man at times. You'll have to learn about him."

Johnny nodded and gulped down the milk. Over lunch he'd already learned a few things that didn't sound too good. The Olaffsons had lived here for twenty years, scratching out a meager living on a river-edge farm. The Mister still kept a horse to pull his plow, and had no use for tractors. There was a bathtub and toilet upstairs—they'd come with the house—but Olaffson had never seen fit to put in plumbing. He sounded like a slave driver who considered hard work the best way to raise a boy.

Johnny had heard of such foster homes before. He'd known one boy who'd been in one. It was simple—people got paid so much to take in a welfare kid and, if they worked him like a dog and fed him cheaply enough, they got a free hired hand and made money on it to boot. He had a cold feeling in the bottom of his stomach as it dawned on him this might be such a home.

The door opened just as Mrs. Olaffson was rinsing the dishes. She fumbled them nervously as Mr. Olaffson walked in. He glanced suspiciously at the milk pitcher on the table, but said nothing. He looked Johnny up and down. "Got work clothes on, boy?"

Johnny nodded.

"Then come on. You can't be setting around here all day. I've got a tool shed to be painted by sundown." He turned and stepped out the door, while Johnny hurried after him.

The tool shed turned out to be a long, low building made of raw lumber. Near one wall sat a five-gallon bucket of red barn paint, and a pair of brushes in a bucket of turpentine. "I've finished the roof. Now you get the walls done. I want it done by dark. My bones tell me it's goin' to rain come mornin'. You know how to paint?"

Johnny nodded, gulping a little as he looked at the long stretch of bare wood waiting for paint. It

20

was a full day's work. "I can't do all—"

"You'd better try," Olaffson said. "It'll be a lot harder doin' it by lantern light after dark. Now get cracking." He walked off heavily, spewing tobacco juice in his wake.

Johnny found an egg crate and, by standing tip-toe on it, managed to reach to the eaves. Standing on it, he painted to either side as far as he could reach. He did one section this way, and his back started to ache. Standing back a moment to survey his progress, he shook his head. *He'd never get it done!*

Slowly the afternoon passed. After a while, Johnny ached in so many places that his body was just one big pain. It was only late May, and the weather was a typical Minnesota spring day, but his T-shirt was dripping with sweat. Finally he just sat down on the egg crate and stared at the wall.

Angrily, he made a round sweep on the wall in front of him. Old man Olaffson sure looked mean. He made a couple of dots in the circle and it began to look like a face. Now a spot for a nose and a big frown, just the way the old man had looked when he'd stamped off and left him to paint. Johnny grinned. A fat moustache now, and he'd have drawn a likeness.

For a moment, the artist in him took over, and a face took shape on the wall. A little line here . . . a shadow there . . . make that line heavier . . . the round sweep of a moustache. He stood up grinning and admired his work. In a rough, slap-dab sort of way, it *did* resemble old man Olaffson at that!

"I didn't set you here to draw funny pictures."

Johnny jumped at the sound. The old man had

21

walked up on him without making any noise. "I was—just resting," Johnny said, dabbing away at the rough sketch, though he was sure the old man had already seen what it was.

"I can see what you need." The old man moved suddenly, faster than Johnny had thought he could, and swung at him with a wide, sweeping blow. Johnny leaped back and crashed into the egg crate.

"You clumsy lout!" the old man bellowed, his Swedish accent more pronounced in his anger. "Look what you done!" Johnny turned to see the pool of red spreading from the tipped-over bucket. "I—I'm sorry," he mumbled, squatting to set it up again. "It was just an accident. Honest!"

Olaffson caught him by the nape of the neck and dragged him to his feet. Johnny winced as the old man slapped him across the mouth. "You need a good strappin'. Take 'em down."

Johnny stared at him, tears in his eyes from the slapping. Then, as the old man unfastened his heavy belt, Johnny understood. "I'll be good. I'll clean it up! Honest! Don't—"

"A crybaby sissy, is that what I got?" The old man flexed the belt in his hand.

Johnny's face froze in anger. "Make me cry!" he spit out. "Just try and make me cry!" He set his teeth, lowered his pants, and turned around. *Just let the old monster make him cry. A sissy, huh? He'd see!*

Whack! Johnny gritted his teeth as the belt dug in. *Whack! Whack!* He felt the tears running down his face and he rubbed them away with paint-stained hands. He wouldn't let the old man see him cry

The old man stepped back. "Now remember this. You've got enough paint left to finish the job. You better work fast to get done by dark. You're not here for a vacation, boy! Don't forget that!"

When darkness fell, there were still twenty feet of the building left to do. And Johnny did them. By lantern light. The old man really *was* that mean. When the last brushful was on, he was so tired and hungry he could hardly move. He dropped the brush wearily into the bucket and started slowly for the house. The ache in his belly was almost as bad as the pain in his back. And the welts from the whipping still ached and throbbed. He realized he hadn't eaten in ten hours, and he was starved.

When he walked into the kitchen, the old man was perched on a high stool, reading a newspaper. "There's your supper," he said, pointing to a small plate of beans on the table. Next to the plate stood a half glass of milk. Johnny stared at the plate. *Why, there was hardly more than a few mouthfuls!*

The old man read his face. "You got to earn your keep around here. That paint what you spilled cost money."

Johnny wanted to answer back but was afraid to. He started to sit down, then jumped up as one of the welts burst. The old man snorted behind his paper.

A few minutes later Johnny gulped down a second glass of water and headed up the stairs for bed. He'd never been so glad to get into bed in his life. He'd just gotten under the covers when the steps creaked and someone pushed his door open softly.

It was Mrs. Olaffson.

She held a finger over her lips for silence and tiptoed lightly over to his bed. "He's odd, the Mister is," she whispered. "It's best not to say much to him." She kissed him on the forehead. "You sleep good now, son." Then she tucked a small package into his hand and slipped out of the room.

Johnny stared after her. *What kind of a place was this?* Then he looked at the package in his hand. It was something in waxed paper. He opened it and found a thick steak between two slices of bread.

A moment later heavy voices in the hallway told him they were having an argument. He ducked the sandwich under his pillow and pretended to be asleep. One sentence in English, mixed with words that must have been Swedish, reached his ears: "But, Nels, the boy must eat...." Then all was quiet.

Long after the sandwich had been eaten and the house lay silent in sleep, Johnny lay there, staring at the wall. *What had he ever done to deserve this?* The tears he had forced back all day finally came. He buried himself under the covers and let them come. He was so mad and frightened and confused he didn't know what to do.

What should he do? Pray? To whom? God? God didn't hear prayers, did He? If He did, then why did He let things like this happen? Why had He let Mom and Dad get a divorce? Why did He let other kids have moms and dads and homes, but not him? Why? Why? He'd tried to pray before, but he never could. Nobody heard. Nobody cared.

But, whatever happened, Johnny knew one thing for sure. He was going to run away. He wouldn't stay here! The first chance he got, no matter what happened. *What had Miss Parsons said? His last chance? So what. Who cared?* Maybe he'd go to the state school, or an orphanage. It didn't matter. Nothing did. Nobody cared what happened. *And he didn't care either!*

The first chance he got, he would run away!

3

Take Me with You, Mom!

THE DAYS slipped past as Johnny learned the routine and rules of life down on the farm. The routine was a simple one: up at the crack of dawn, eat, and work. Breakfast was usually mush or dry cereal and toast. One morning Mrs. Olaffson had fried him eggs, but the old man had walked in then and given her a tongue-lashing on the price of eggs. And that had finished that.

Out in the barn, the main thing was to keep out of Olaffson's way and get the morning chores done—right and fast. That meant milking seven cows, and it took Johnny only one session with the belt to learn that milking wasn't half as hard as it looked. Then four hundred hens had to be fed with corn ground up in the cobber. And eight baskets had to be filled with eggs. The first day he broke three eggs, and got three neat, mechanical cuffs on the ear. After that, he buried the remains of any he broke.

Then the hogs had to be slopped and the barn cleaned, which meant shoveling out the twin troughs, hauling out the manure without spilling any, and hosing the floor down.

By then it was nine o'clock and the work for the day could really begin. One day it might be forty rows of tomatoes to be weeded, the next a whole shedful of plows, harrows, rakes, and discs to be oiled. Johnny didn't know how to do it, but he knew he'd better do a good job anyway. So he just oiled every hole he could find and still got whipped—for breaking the handle on the grease gun.

The old man hated two things—talking and idle hands. And he had a single remedy for both of them, as well as anything else that displeased him. After a week, Johnny was so sore from work, and so bruised and welted up from whippings, that he was just glad to get in bed at night and lie there safe for a few hours at least.

The days passed slowly, tallied up as so many slaps, whippings, and blisters, so many meals of mush, potatoes, stewed tomatoes, and beans. On Sundays he got meat. To most people, Sunday was a day of rest. To Johnny it was just another workday, but he got meat. Hamburger, usually. "Meat costs money," the old man grunted. "We ain't rich folks like you're used to in the city, boy."

Clothes cost money too, he learned. It was just past noon, on his second Tuesday there, and he was hurrying to get done by lunch. He was nailing planks on the stove-in back wall of the hen house, and, in his hurry to finish, he turned around too fast and caught his pants on a nail. He groaned as he heard the *Rrrrippp!* that meant his one good pair of jeans was torn wide open. Then he heard a "Stupid lout!" and looked up to see the old man, suddenly standing right before him.

Johnny gulped at him, then looked down at his ripped trousers. "It—it was—an accident. Honest!"

"Got any more overalls? Clean?"

"Just an old pair. But they're dirty. I didn't mean to—"

The old man fingered his belt. "Them pants cost good money. You know that, boy?"

Johnny shrugged. "I'm supposed to get new clothes this month anyway. The welfare sends you a check to pay for them, don't they? I know they do. So I can get new overalls."

The old man's face went white. "Don't you be worrying about no check! That's my business, not for some welfare brat to lip off to me about! You need to be taught not to rip your pants. I gotta teach you better, I guess."

"No!" Johnny shouted defiantly, not caring what happened anymore. "It was an accident! You ain't supposed to whip me. I'm gonna tell Miss Parsons on you! I'm gonna tell everything!" He jumped back, watching the old man, ready to run. *He won't whip me again! I'll run away, right now!*

The old man stepped forward, swinging the belt in his hand. "I guess I gotta give you a real whippin', boy. I'll teach you to lip off to your betters!"

Just then the crunch of tires on gravel reached

29

them and they looked up to see a car pulling into the driveway. Johnny stared at it, then shouted in relief. "My mom! It's my mother. She's come to visit me!"

"Eh?" the old man said, staring at the car warily. It was a flashy blue convertible, with a black-haired man and a pretty, red-haired woman in a white dress in the front seat. "Your mother, you say?"

"That's her boyfriend George's car. He must of brought her to see me." Johnny stared at the old man hard. *He wouldn't dare to whip him now!*

Olaffson rubbed his chin thoughtfully, then started putting his belt back on. "You got one coming," he said in a low voice, his eyes cold and black. "Don't think I'll be forgettin' it."

Johnny heard him, but he didn't care. He was safe now that his mom was here. And he *would* tell on the old man. *Everything!*

Mom was on the porch talking to Mrs. Olaffson when he came running up to the house. She had her good-smelling perfume on, and she hugged him for a long time before letting him go. "We just happened to be driving out this way; so we thought we'd stop by and see how you're getting along in your new home."

"He's doing just fine," Mrs. Olaffson said. "I was just telling your mother about the new calf, Johnny." She looked at him for a moment, and Johnny thought he detected a strange look on her face. She glanced over toward the barn, and he saw the old man standing there watching them. "Johnny just thrives on this outdoor life, don't you, son?"

Johnny nodded. "It's—it's pretty different, that's for sure." *Why, she was afraid! She was afraid he'd say the wrong thing—and—she was afraid of the old man too!*

"Can we go and—and get a malt?" Johnny asked. "There's a dairy stand about a half mile up the road, I think. Is it OK, Mrs. Olaff—"

She looked over at the old man, then back at Johnny. "Why—why, yes. By all means." She looked at Mom. "But don't be gone too long now. The Mister, he's an odd one." She patted Johnny absently on the head and walked quickly back into the house.

George was all smiles. "Hi, sport! he said as

Johnny got in the back seat. "How do you like farm life?"

"I don't," Johnny said. "I hate it here. I want to leave this place right away!" He looked at his mother. "The old man was gonna whip me again, just when you drove up."

Mother refused to get upset. "Whip you? What did you do?"

"Nothin'! He just whips me all the time, for nothing at all!"

George turned the car around and drove slowly up to the highway. "It doesn't seem as if the old coot would whip you, unless you went and did something, now does it?" He winked at Mom. "I think the boy's got a case of hippikanorus of the hyphodomanater, huh?"

That was something George liked to say, and Johnny knew it was supposed to be funny. But he didn't feel like laughing. His mother had been going with George about a year, but Johnny had never really liked him. He seemed like a big phony, always smoking a big cigar and talking big talk, with his hair all slicked down. Once Johnny had heard him make a crack to his mother about his dad being a drunk. He knew *that* was the real reason he didn't like him.

"Why did Mr. Olaffson whip you?" Mom asked. "You know, you've got a bad habit of talking back to grown-ups. You ask for a spanking a lot of the time."

"Whose side are you on?" Johnny said, halfway shouting. "Don't you even *care* what happens to me? LOOK! Just look at this!" He pulled his T-shirt up over his head, revealing a pair of welts on his back from the whipping he'd gotten over the broken grease gun.

"He could of got those falling out of a tree," George said. "Anyway, a good spankin' now and then's good for a growin' boy. Makes a man out of him."

"I don't think Mr. Olaffson would whip you if you hadn't *done* something," Mom said. "The welfare is pretty careful. Anyway, we came to have a little fun together, didn't we? There's the drive-in now. Let's all get malts and just enjoy ourselves."

"YOU DON'T CARE!" Johnny shouted, threatening to break into tears at any moment. "The old man could beat me all day and—and you—you just wouldn't give a damn!" He broke into open sobbing. "You don't care what happens to me!"

"Johnny!" Mother was plainly shocked, as much by what he said as by the language he'd used. "You don't mean that. You can't! You know that's not so!"

George eased into the parking space in the drive-in and turned around to face Johnny. "You watch your mouth! You shouldn't ever say a thing like that to your mother! I may not be your father, but—"

"No, you ain't my father!" Johnny shouted, tears streaming down his face. "And I'm glad you ain't! If you was, I'd jump under a train. Don't you try to tell me what to do!"

"Johnny, what's the *matter* with you?" Mother said, her face plainly troubled and real concern in her eyes now. George went for malts while she got in the back with him. "Tell me, what's wrong?"

"Mom, take me with you! Please! I just want to go away, and live like other kids—in a *real home!* I don't want to go back there. Don't make me! Take me with you. Please!"

"Honey, I can't." Mom's voice was soft and low. "You know I just can't do anything. That's the law." She rocked him back and forth in her arms. "I want you to come with me as bad as you want to go but, honey, I can't do anything. You know I want to."

Johnny sniffed and rubbed his eyes. "I—I guess I should have known not to ask," he said. "I know it too. But—but sometimes I just want to be like other kids so much, that I—"

"I'm sorry, honey," Mom said. "And so is George."

George came back with the malts and slipped in the back seat. "Friends, sport?"

Johnny tried a lopsided grin. "Yeah. I'm sorry, I—"

"That's okay," George said. "I suppose it does get pretty lonesome out on the farm with those old folks sometimes." He handed him a malt and a hamburger. "Does the old man really knock you around?"

Johnny nodded. "He gets pretty mean sometimes."

"I'll report it to the agency, if he really does whip you without any real reason," Mom said. "Maybe I better have a talk with—"

"No, don't say anything to him," Johnny broke in. "He'll just whip me for telling you. I know he will!"

George's smile vanished as quickly as it had

come. "Maybe he's afraid the old man will tell you something he doesn't want you to find out."

"No! That's not it! You just don't know how mean he is."

"I'm going to have a talk with him, John," Mother said, and Johnny knew she meant it. "If you haven't done anything wrong, then you don't have anything to worry about. Now, let's have our malts in peace."

That spoiled the afternoon. *If you haven't done anything wrong, then you don't have anything to worry about.* It sounded nice, and he'd heard grown-ups say it a hundred times. But Johnny knew it was a lie.

A half hour later, sitting on the old mohair sofa in the living room while Mom talked with the old man in the kitchen, he knew just how big a lie it was. Mom wasn't smiling when she came out. "I'm glad you told me the whole story," she was saying. "I used to have the same trouble with him when he was little." She looked at Johnny and shook her head. "You do what you think best," she told the old man.

Johnny got up to kiss her good-bye, and she just brushed his cheek. "Johnny, Johnny," she said. "When are you going to learn to take your medicine like a man? You're getting more like your father—" She stopped suddenly, aware that she had said the wrong thing. Johnny went cold to her touch.

"Don't you talk about Dad! He's the one who loves me, not you! You believe all the lies people tell you about me!"

"Well, Mr. Olaffson told me—"

"He told you stories he made up," Johnny said. "I never did a thing to get whipped for. He just told you lies to make you think I did!"

"You best be respectful, son," Mr. Olaffson said, taking him by the arm so hard that Johnny almost cried out in pain. "I'll have a talk with the lad, Mrs. Nolan. Everything will be just fine."

"You try to behave then, Johnny," Mom said, backing out the door "I'll drop you a letter later this week." And then she was gone, and he was alone with the old man.

"So you think you're mistreated, eh, boy?" The old man started unbuckling his belt. "You think they'd treat you better in the boys' school, where the likes of you belong? If it wasn't for decent folks like me taking you in—"

"What did you tell her?" Johnny said, not caring what happened anymore. "You lied to her to make her hate me!"

"Never you mind," Olaffson said. "You just worry about a welfare brat who won't be able to sit down for a week." Then he whirled Johnny around and yanked his pants down. The belt cut into him harder than it ever had before, and Johnny screamed in pain. After the fourth or fifth time, Mrs. Olaffson ran into the room, shouting, "Nels! You'll cripple the boy!"

But the old man waved her off while he finished the job. He left Johnny leaning over the sofa, sobs choking his throat, burning arrows of pain shooting through him. "I want you out in the fields in ten minutes," he said, stamping out of the room.

Mrs. Olaffson scurried in with a pan of soapy water and washed him off. She wiped mineral oil and lard into two places the belt had broken the skin, and taped them up. "The Mister, sometimes he frightens me, son," she said. "I'm sorry, but he won't listen to what I say."

"That's all right," Johnny said. "I don't blame you." *And you won't have to do this again,* he vowed, walking out to work a few minutes later. *Because I won't be here!* Three days to go, not counting today. On Saturday the old man would crank up the Ford and go to Hastings to sit in the barbershop while the Mrs. did the shopping. *And this week, when they get back, I won't be here!*

4

Let's Run Away Together

THE NEXT morning when he came down to breakfast, Johnny was surprised to see a plate heaped
high with sausages, eggs, and fried potatoes sitting
on the table. Next to it sat glasses of orange juice
and milk and a basket of hot rolls. "You just eat
good now, son," Mrs. Olaffson said, "and let me
worry about the Mister. Enough is enough."

After breakfast the chores went fast and the
only time the old man came around to check on him
he said, "Good morning, lad," in such a smiling way
that Johnny almost dropped the basket of eggs he
was toting. By the time he came in for lunch that
noon, it was pretty clear that something odd was
going on. He'd tipped over a half bucket of milk,
and all the old man had said was, "Better clean it
up before it fetches in the mice."

And when he found a plate of pork chops waiting for him at lunch, Johnny didn't know what to think. He just ate and wondered. After dinner, the old man called him out on the porch and pointed through the window down toward the river bottom a half mile away. "A right pretty sight from here, don't you think? Man oughta look at things like that sometimes."

"Eerr, yeah, it is quite a view," Johnny said, stuffing his hands in his pockets and feeling awkward. He stared with the old man, following the sweep of his hand down to where the sandstone bluffs fell away to a black mud flat and merged with the river. There was one point in particular, a sharp jut of sandy ground dotted with boulders and swamp oak that was a ready-made landscape, just crying to be painted.

"You draw some, don't you?"

"A little. Watercolors, mostly."

"My oldest boy was a great one for drawin' pictures. You see that picture of a big bay stallion on the parlor wall? He done that."

"No kiddin?" That's pretty good drawing."

"Yep, two boys I had. Both growed and gone away now." The old man stood staring out the window. "Been near to twenty years since I saw either of them. They just signed into the Navy, and never come back. The oldest's in California. He sends Mother a card every Christmas. He's the one who done the picture. The other never did write."

The old man stared in silence a while longer, then turned to him. "You got any drawin' stuff?"

"In my room."

"Maybe you oughta go down by the river and see if you can't make a nice picture. Something to hang on the wall."

"But—but, ain't I supposed to weed that—"

"It can wait. You go and draw. Take all afternoon if you like. A boy can't work all the time." Then the old man turned quickly and hurried out of the room, slamming the door as he left the house. Johnny stared after him, then turned and mounted the stairs to his room. *Boy, but life got mixed up at times! Life,* he thought, *and people!*

The sun was already balancing on a rim of hills when he slowly made his way back over the slope just south of the farm that afternoon. And Johnny was proud of himself. He'd never done better work than this, especially the top picture on his sketchbook, the jut of land that had first caught his eye from the house. The old man had wanted something to hang on the wall, hadn't he? Well, this was it!

Suddenly he felt happy. But, as he came into the farmyard, an odd feeling came over him. *Something was wrong!* Walking slowly into the yard, he stared around as if he could *see* the reason for the odd feeling. And then, in the shadow between the barn and the silo, he saw the reason.

The reason turned out to be a boy, older than himself, standing in the shadow and smoking a cigarette. He seemed to be keeping a nervous eye on the house. Then he turned, saw Johnny, and grinned in a cocky way, the cigarette dangling from a corner of his mouth. He was quite a bit bigger than Johnny, husky, with thick black hair, and the trace of a beard just starting to show. Walking over, Johnny realized that he had one of *his* shirts on—the blue one Dad gave him last Christmas.

"Hi! I'm Pete Dexter. You must be Johnny Nolan, huh, kid?"

Johnny stared at him. "I, err, yeah, that is—"

"Where'd I come from? The old battle-ax brung me down this afternoon. She asked about you. The old geezer said you was off drawin' pictures."

"Parsons?" Johnny said, setting his paint box and sketch pad on an upended egg crate. "My case-worker? Was she here today?"

"Didn't you know? She went to get me this morning and brought me out here."

"What, that dirty, rotten no-good—" Johnny's face went sheet-white. *So that was why the old man had sent him off painting! And that explained the breakfast, and the pork chops, and everything! The old man had known all along that Miss Parsons was coming, and wanted him to be gone when she came! So he couldn't tell her about him!*

He turned around and kicked the egg basket as hard as he could. His paint box went sailing, followed by a cluster of brushes. Then he snatched up the sketch pad and ripped it in half, and half again, throwing the pieces around the yard. "That dirty, rotten, sneaky— He knew! He knew all—"

"Hey, kid, don't flip your lid!" Pete grabbed him by the shoulders. He was stronger than he looked, almost as strong as a man, Johnny noted. "Take a break. What's the big beef?"

"He knew she was bringing you here all the time!" He looked up at Pete. "They were afraid I'd

41

tell her. And, hey, you're smokin'," he added, almost as an afterthought. "And that's my shirt you got on. How old are you, anyway?"

"Fifteen, and I smoke when I feel like it," Pete said. "And I hope you ain't mad about the shirt. I ain't got no clothes, except the state job stuff they give me at Lafayette."

"Lafayette? You mean—"

"The *joint*, kid," Pete said. "The Boys' Industrial School." He flexed his arm, showing off a home-made tattoo of a heart with wings and a ribbon across it reading: *B.I.S.—PETE*. "All the right guys at Laffie got these. You want a tattoo? I can make a good one if you ain't chicken."

"Me? Naw." Then Johnny saw the look on Pete's face. "Well, maybe later, huh?" *Well, why not?* "What were you in there for, anyway?"

"To get a replacement. I been in and out since I was nine. My people are kinda messed up. I was just back while they dug up a new farm placement to parole me to. I kinda cornballed the last one I had."

"Cornballed?"

"Messed up, you know?" Pete took a long drag on the cigarette. "Man, are you a dope! Yeah, the old man there thought he was bad. He got all salty with me and I had to deck him." He cracked a fist into his palm. "I showed him not to push me around."

"So they put you here now, huh?" Johnny said, still a little awed. He'd never met a guy like Pete, up close anyway, in his whole life.

"I'm here, ain't I? And I hear this is a creep joint. I know a dude was here a year ago. He said

42

the old man whipped up on him all the time."

Johnny nodded. "He went to town on me last night. And it wasn't the first time either."

"That so? Well, I plan on breezin' out of this dump pretty quick. Maybe I'll take you along, if you don't chicken out. You wanta go too?"

Johnny opened his mouth to answer. Then suddenly, he saw the old man step around the silo, behind Pete. "Hey, uhh—"

"Smoke, do you?" the old man said in a loud voice, whirling Pete around and pushing him against the barn. "Not on my farm you don't." Then he back-handed him and sent the butt flying, while Pete went sprawling against the silo.

"And you—" He looked at Johnny, and there was no trace of the friendliness he'd shown that noon. "You better clean up that mess." He pointed at the remains of his sketchbook. "Then I want the front yard hosed down and hay thrown down for the horses. There'll be sandwiches on the table till—" he looked at his watch—"till seven-forty-five. So you better get crackin'. Lights out at eight tonight. Lots of tomatoes to weed tomorrow."

He turned and walked off quickly, leaving Johnny staring after him, while Pete leaned against the silo rubbing his jaw. "I see what you mean. He's a mean old geezer, ain't he? But just let him try it when I'm lookin'." He flexed his fist and shook it after the departing figure. "Try it when I'm ready for you, you old rat." But Johnny noticed that the old man was far out of hearing by then.

They made it to bed just as the old pendulum

43

clock in the hall struck eight. Johnny lay there, next to Pete, waiting until he was sure he could hear the old man snoring. Then he whispered, "Did you mean it? I mean about running away together?"

"Yeah, man," Pete said. "Wanta go?"

"I was gonna go anyhow," Johnny said.

"Good." Pete rubbed his chin. "How long you been here?"

"A couple weeks, almost. I just moved here from a place in the Cities. I been in lots of these places. This is my twelfth. How many you been in?"

"I don't know," Pete said. "I did a lot of time in Laffie. Then I lived with my uncle when I run off once. But they caught me and took me back."

"What about your folks?"

Pete grunted. "My old man's in the penitentiary. He's a burglar—the cops just got lucky and nailed him. And my ma—well, I don't know where she is. Out on the bricks someplace, I guess. I don't know, and I don't care."

"My folks got divorced about five years ago," Johnny said. "And the welfare took me. Only my aunt pays the Wentworth Home to handle me."

"My old man paid in advance for me before he got busted," Pete said. "He don't work much, but when he does, the pay is good." He laughed. "I'm gonna be better'n him, though. I kicked in lots of places. I got two hundred out of a drugstore once."

"Stealin'?" Johnny said. "You steal?"

"What are you— simple? Everybody steals. Didn't you ever cop something? Even a bike? Just for fun? Sometimes I take cars, and just bomb around in them, like I own them."

"No, guess I never did. But I ain't scared to, if that's what you think. I just—" He shrugged.

"They was talkin' about your dad today. Parsons and them. Said he just got out of the hospital. She

45

said he was a dipso—whatchacallit. It means he's a winehead, I guess."

Johnny sat up suddenly, his fists balling in anger. *"He ain't! Don't you say that! He ain't!"*

"Lighten up, kid!" Pete said, grabbing him by the shoulders and pushing him back on the bed. "Forget it. It ain't no big thing. Let's talk about something important, like blowin' this dump. Does the old man ever leave you alone here?"

Johnny stared at the ceiling, waiting for his anger to subside. He knew it was dangerous to get mad at Pete, who'd think nothing of punching him.

"I said lighten up," Pete said, gripping his arm tightly. "I'm sorry I said that. Okay?"

"All right," Johnny said. "But don't say that again. And, yeah, the old man takes her to town every Saturday to shop."

"In a car? Has he got an old car in that garage?"

"An old VW. Why?"

"Just curious." Pete rubbed his chin. "Saturday, huh? Yeah, that sounds like a winner. Three days to go then. Let's shake on it."

"Shake!" Johnny took his hand, grinning.

But sleep was a long time in coming. Pete wasn't his idea of the kind of guy he wanted to be. But, anyway, he *was* on his side. He knew what it was like. He wasn't like all the other kids, with their moms and dads and homes and all. *He's on my side!*

Besides, he didn't have to steal or do anything wrong, just cause Pete did, did he? They'd just run off and then—then—just see what happened. That wasn't important. What was important was that, in just three days, he and Pete were going to run away!

5

Let Me Out!

WHEN the old man had said "lots of tomatoes to weed tomorrow," he had really meant it. The work turned out to be the hardest Johnny had done since coming to the farm. Before the sun was halfway up the sky, his shirt was soaked with sweat. "Hey, hot enough for you?" he yelled over to Pete who was leaning on a hoe a few feet up the next row.

"I like it hot. And this ain't nothin' compared to runnin' the coal pile at Laffie."

"What's that?"

"When you mess up there, they stick you in H Cottage, that's Hudson House. And every day you put in five hours carrying coal to the power plant. You gotta run about one hundred feet with it and use big shovels. They make you run too, and a lot of guys drop."

"What happens to them?"

"Punks like that get kicked in the head. Everybody runs by and throws a scoop of coal on them."

"What about the guard, or—"

"The man?" Pete laughed. "He just looks the other way. And if the fink goes to the man and snitches, then we have court up in the dormitory at night. If you get known as a snitch, man, you're in trouble. Down there, you got to be able to duke a little, or guys lean on you. The more guys you can whip, the more bully you got. I had third bully in the whole joint; so nobody messed with me."

Johnny stripped off his T-shirt and tucked it into his waistband. "Well, old man Olaffson got the bully here; so we better get back to work."

Pete grunted. "When's he want this done?"

"Tonight. He'll be out to check on us too."

"Tonight? He's nuts!"

"Maybe," Johnny admitted. "But he's the man here, right?"

Pete dug in with his hoe. "We'll work today and tomorrow, but Saturday—" He looked around carefully, to make sure the old man was nowhere in sight. "Saturday I'll be the man here, right?"

"Right!" He looked toward the barn on a hunch, and saw the old man, just coming out of the barn. "There's the old whatchamacallit now."

They both bent over their hoes, chopping away.
Saturday, Johnny thought. *Saturday!*

The long day wore on, dully, mechanically.
Chop, bend, pull. Chop, bend, pull. Lunchtime came and went in silence. While the long afternoon wore

48

on, Johnny's hands did the work automatically, while his mind raced furiously, thinking, thinking, thinking! Once he looked up from his work to see Pete, squatting down behind a heavy cluster of weeds at the end of one row, sneaking a cigarette. "Want a drag?" he offered.

"Naw, I guess not," Johnny said.

"Well, keep cases for me, all right?"

"Keep what?"

"*Cases*, man," Pete said impatiently. "Watch for the man, dummy!"

Johnny grunted and slowly pecked away at the weeds with his hoe, keeping one eye peeled on the farm buildings. He sneaked a look over at Pete, trying to figure out what he saw. He saw a boy who was big at fifteen, dark, and husky. A boy who walked with a cocky shuffle, swaggering his shoulders. A boy who never seemed to smile, just smirk. A boy he didn't like.

He wondered for a moment if it was really a smart move he was making—to run away with Pete. *Still, what choice did he have?* He shook his head. *Things would turn out all right. Somehow.*

But he didn't like Pete and he knew it. Especially, he didn't like the way Pete just took over, seeming to assume he'd do whatever Pete told him to. He was wearing one of his shirts again, and he hadn't even asked till after he had it on.

Johnny caught sight of the old man, glaring down at them along the row, and decided that a lot worse things could happen than running away with Pete. *Like staying here all summer.*

"There he is," Johnny said.

Pete stepped on the butt and popped up, hoe in hand. "Thanks, kid. You'll be all right. You just need old Pete showin' you the ropes is all. Just listen to me, kid, and you'll be havin' a ball before you know it."

"We better look busy."

Pete glanced up at the old man. "Yeah, the old rat." He tacked on a string of profanity and began hacking away at weeds.

"Hey," Johnny whispered. "When we take off, ya know—well, where do you think we oughta go?"

"St. Paul, where else?" Pete said. "I know some good guys there."

"But—but that's *thirty* miles away. I mean, how do we get there?"

Pete gave him a slow grin and winked. "Just stick with Pete, kid. That's my problem, and I'll take care of it."

Johnny nodded, but he wasn't convinced. *Still, what choice have I got? What else can I do? Nothing. Nothing at all.* He'd just have to see what Saturday brought, and the days after.

Friday came and went as another fourteen-hour session bent over a hoe in the tomato patch. And, before Johnny realized it, it was Saturday afternoon, and he and Pete were already half through with the day's work. *Tonight's the night!* Johnny thought.

Both the Olaffsons had gone into town just after lunch to do the shopping for the week. The old man had left him and Pete with orders to finish the south patch of tomatoes by the time they got back, eight o'clock, he thought it would be. *Just at dark,*

Johnny thought, looking up at the sky. *It must be almost six right now.* He was so excited he felt like jumping up and down.

"We could go right now, you know that?" he said to Pete, stopping work long enough to see they'd never be finished by dark. *But it didn't matter! Not a bit.* "If we went right now, we'd have a couple hours head start."

"Naw." Pete gave him a hard look. "I *told* you— we go when *I* say we go. And *I* say we wait till after dark, after they're back. I got me a little idea." He poked in his Levi's and fished out a crumpled pack of cigarettes. "Take a break and have a butt with me."

Johnny hesitated, then saw the slightly sneering look on Pete's face. *Well, why not? He wasn't a little kid now, was he?* "Sure, I might as well," he said, trying to sound as though smoking was something he did now and then, when he felt like it. He took the cigarette while Pete lit a match. The first drag went down all right, but the second one caught in his windpipe and he broke into a fit of coughing.

"Oh, no!" Pete snickered. "Man, you just can't do nothin' right, can you?" He lit his own. "You got no cool, Johnny-boy. Just take it slow and easy like this. You don't have to inhale till you're used to it. See?"

Johnny followed Pete's example closely and managed to take a few more drags without coughing again. But the smoke made him dizzy and he got got an odd, quivery feeling in his stomach. Very carefully he butted the cigarette on his shoe and put the stub in his pocket. "I'll save this for later."

51

"Go ahead," Pete said. "It takes a while. You just stick with old Pete and I'll teach you all you gotta know."

"It'll be dark soon," Johnny said, looking skyward. "Are you sure we—"

"I told you once," Pete said. "Now, you just be cool, dig?"

Johnny nodded, grinning more out of fear than ease. "Okay, man, I'm with you. Dig?"

"Hey, that's my Johnny-boy," Pete said. "That's more like it."

Darkness came with no sight of a returning car, and they went to sit in a tool shed, between the garage and the barn, to wait. Pete was digging around in a bin of old parts. "What you lookin' for?" Johnny asked. "Maybe I can help you."

"Got it," Pete said, tucking something into the waistband of his pants. Johnny saw the bulge under his shirt and looked at him quizzically. "Forget it," Pete said, boosting himself up on the crossbeam of the harrow next to Johnny. "You really ready to go now?"

"You bet," Johnny said.

Pete lit a cigarette and held the lit match out. "You got a butt, ain't you?"

Hastily Johnny dug out his butt and took a couple drags before throwing it away. He didn't like smoking after all, he decided.

"Now, you do just as I tell you," Pete said. "You better not chicken out on me or it'll be too bad for you. You understand that real good now?" He took Johnny's arm and squeezed hard.

"Hey—oww!" Johnny yelped. "That hurts, Pete!

Cut it out, huh?"

Pete let him go. "Just want to let you know what'll happen if you turn yellow on me now. I'm going through with this, all the way, and you better just shut up and do what I say or else." He cracked his fist into the palm of his hand in demonstration. "Hey, ain't that a car now?"

Johnny held a hand over his ear, then saw the reflection of the lights against the barn wall. "Yeah, here they come now."

Pete stuck his hand inside his shirt, gripping some unseen object. "Okay, you sit right here, and don't move till I say, understand?" He eased up to the door, peeking out, then waved Johnny over. The old Ford puttered down the driveway and headed into the open garage. A moment later, burdened down with packages, Mrs. Olaffson went lumbering for the house.

"I'm going out to check on the boys," the old man said. "I'll be back to carry in the heavy stuff in a moment." He turned and started walking for the barn. Pete and Johnny ducked back out of sight as he walked past the open door of the shed.

Once he had passed, Pete took hold of Johnny's shoulder and said in a low voice: "You slip over to the garage now and get in the car and wait for me."

"In the car? But—but you ain't gonna—"

"I said you get in the car and wait for me!" Pete hissed. "You understand?" He increased the pressure on Johnny's shoulder. "Now get over there, and quick! And don't let the old man see you!"

Johnny nodded, gulping, and went. In the early darkness, it was easy to slip over and ease into the

53

garage unseen. He stealthily opened the door and got into the front seat, on the right-hand side. *Was Pete planning to steal the car? Or what? I'm not a thief!* Johnny told himself. *I'm not a thief! What kind of a mess have I gotten myself into anyway?*

He slouched down on the seat, as though he could make himself invisible, and noticed that his hands were shaking. He was scared, more scared than he remembered ever having been. *What if I get caught? Well, what if I do? Who would care, really? Nobody. Why should I? What does it matter? I'll show them. They'll see now!* "I'll show you, all of you!" he said, half aloud. But he knew, deep down, he was lying.

Suddenly he heard voices outside, muffled noises, something that sounded like a scream, and running footsteps. A moment later the car door flew open and Pete jumped in, panting heavily. He flipped something onto the floor, and Johnny heard keys jingling. "Hang on, kid. Here we go!"

And before Johnny really knew what was happening, Pete jammed a key into the ignition and the car roared to life.

"What! What happened, Pete? Are you—" He stared about wildly, half in fear, half in excitement.

"Shut up! Just shut up and hang on!"

The car whipped back out of the garage, then spun in a wild arc around the farmyard. A moment later they roared up the dirt road, then spun out onto the highway in a spray of spun gravel. Then they were racing down the dark highway, the old VW gently swaying from side to side. The speedometer needle rocked between seventy and eighty.

"Whee hoo!" Pete yelled, bursting into laughter. "Man! we got it made. The old man still don't know what hit him!"

"Hit him? You—" And then Johnny saw Pete flick his eyes down to the floorboards for a moment. He followed them and found a length of lead pipe. He picked it up but dropped it quickly when he felt the end wet and sticky with fresh blood.

"You—you hit him!" He stared at Pete, terror struck. *He hadn't counted on anything like this!* "No—I didn't—"

"Just a love tap," Pete said. "We needed some bread, didn't we? Man, I got his whole wad. Dig this!" He reached inside his shirt and flipped a wallet

over to Johnny. "See how much there is. We can use it more than the old rat could."

Johnny picked up the wallet, staring at it in horror. *What had he gotten himself in for? He didn't want any part of this.* "No!" he screamed. "No! Let me out! I don't want to go now!"

"What?" Pete roared. "Turning yellow, punk? Why, you gutless little fink. You can't chicken out now. Give me the wallet, you yellow little punk!"

"No! No!" Johnny echoed, clutching the wallet. "Stop the car and let me out!"

"Give me the wallet. You ain't going anyplace I'm gonna beat some sense into you, soon as we get far enough away to stop. Now, give me that wallet!"

The wind whipping in from the open window gave him an idea. He held the wallet up, balancing it on the edge of the half-raised glass. "I'll throw it out the window! Honest I will! Let me out or I'll throw it out the window, Pete!"

"Why, you phony little punk! Gimme that!" Pete reached over, making a grab for the wallet, and his hands slipped from the wheel for an instant.

"Look out!" Johnny screamed. "Look out—"

But it was too late. He could feel the car tilting to one side as Pete lunged back, wrestling with the wheel, trying to keep the car under control. "Help! God, help!" Pete screamed.

And then Johnny saw the world tilt crazily and his head slammed into something hard. A crashing sound filled his head, and he thought he saw Pete floating across the windshield.

And then all was still and black.

6

I'll Get Sent Up, Huh?

SO THIS *is what jail looked like.* Johnny sat up on
the narrow bed, yawning, and looked around. It was
just a big, dirty room with three walls of concrete,
smeared with green paint, etched with hundreds of
initials. The fourth wall was all bars, painted black,
with a sliding barred door. From a tiny window, high
up the back wall, a square of sunlight floated through
the grimy frosted glass. It was Sunday morning.

Nine o'clock? Or ten? I wonder. . . . He flipped
his legs over the side of the bed, noticing that he'd
been sleeping on the filthy ticking of a thin, lumpy
mattress. He looked for his shoes, then remembered
vaguely someone taking them off him. He looked
around slowly. The room was almost empty. Two
narrow steel cots, with mattresses folded back, sat
along the other wall. At the head of his bed stood

a gray steel table and three green steel stools. Under the window was a greasy tin sink and a battered dispenser of paper cups. A foul-smelling toilet gurgled in the corner.

So this is jail...when do we eat? He realized then that he was hungry. *It must be morning... wish I could see out the window...is that church bells?* He heard a *scuttle-scuttle* and turned to watch a shiny cockroach maneuvering across the wall. He wanted to throw a pillow at it, but saw that he didn't have one.

He yawned again and lay back, his hands folded under his head, staring up at the ceiling. It was ten feet high and covered with years of dirt. It had once been green, a long time ago. He tried to read the scramble of names and dates scratched up there, but was able to make out only one inscription through the dirt: *ROCKY WARREN—The World's Tallest Burglar Was Here.* He grinned, wondering how he'd managed to get up there. *So this was jail.* It wasn't so bad at that.

He crossed his legs, and that was when he first realized just how sore he was. He ached all over. And his arm was still sore from the shot he'd gotten. He looked at the tiny red swelling, remembering the excitement of the past night. He'd never forget that as long as he lived.

After the crash the first noise had been Pete yowling. He'd found himself just outside the car, on the road, and Pete in a ditch. Then he'd seen the red lights of police cars and heard the wail of an ambulance. He must have passed out then...blank-

ness . . . dim noises. Then he remembered a noisy hospital ward . . . people asking questions . . . a doctor who smelled of stale cigars, examining him . . . a nurse giving him a shot . . . and a happy, relaxed, dull, and listless feeling. He'd started laughing quietly. He remembered a loud voice saying, "They aren't hurt, neither one of them. Just shook up. You can lock them up if you want to." Then someone had led him to a squad car. He remembered Pete being dragged past, screaming. Then a gray building . . . bars . . . and the narrow bed he was lying on now. . . .

"Are you hungry, lad?"

"Huh?" Johnny sat up, startled out of his daydreaming by the sudden voice.

The jailer, a short, fat, greasy-looking man with steel-rimmed glasses, stood outside the door balancing a tray on one arm while he juggled the big key in the lock. "How you feelin' today?"

"Okay, I guess," Johnny said. "What time is it?"

"Noon. You got an appointment?" The jailer winked. "You may as well sit easy. You're apt to be here a few days—till Tuesday at least, if I get my guess. You're welfare. The other'n is goin' back in the mornin'."

"Pete?"

"Him," the jailer said, setting the steel tray on the steel table and fishing a steel spoon out of his shirt pocket. He wiped it on his shirt sleeve and buried it, handle upright, in the mashed potatoes. "Yep. Just got a call on him now. Lafayette's sending a man down to pick him up in the morning. He's just lucky the old man wasn't hurt bad, or he mighta got bound over to district court."

"He's only fifteen," Johnny said. "And I'm not thirteen yet."

"You'd a gone to Lafayette, but he coulda gone up to the joint. I seen 'em go up there before at fifteen. Learn 'em. But Olaffson wasn't hurt bad."

"I'm glad of that," Johnny said.

"Are you now, boy?"

"No, maybe I ain't. Maybe I lied."

The jailer shrugged. "Most folks here do. Lie to me, that is. You eat up now. No more till six tonight. This ain't no hotel." He walked out and left Johnny with his thoughts.

So the old man hadn't been hurt bad. That was lucky. Johnny felt odd. It scared him to realize he hadn't given a thought to what happened to the old man. *He wasn't like that, was he? Like Pete?* He'd never known he could be that heartless. He tried to push the thoughts aside and sat down to eat.

It looked better than the jail meals he'd seen in movies on TV—a mound of potatoes, gravy, peas, a slab of ham, salad, bread, butter—and even a big scoop of strawberry ice cream. *Jail wasn't so bad at that—not yet, anyway.*

The long afternoon dragged. He tried to sleep, but he wasn't tired. He walked around, but that wore out in a hurry. He tried rolling his socks up into a ball and bouncing them off the wall. But that was boring. He tried to whistle, but gave it up. Then he began looking for something to read. Anything.

Crumpled up under the table, as though someone had flung it there a month ago, he found a battered Gideon Bible. *Better than nothing.* He sat down on the edge of the cot and opened it.

FRISCO PETE—King of the Boosters someone had lettered on the inside front cover in red ink. Below that was a drawing of a skull with a snake writhing around it, and a banner reading: *Death Before Dishonor.*

He thumbed through it idly. *Could he still recite all the books in order?* He remembered learning them in Bible camp three summers ago, when the Carlsons had sent him away so that they could go on a trip. He made it as far as Ruth and gave up. He flipped to Luke and read three verses, then threw the book on the floor. *Religion—what good was it? What had God ever done for him?* The book lay open at Psalms. Johnny picked it up and read: *"O give thanks unto the Lord; for He is good...." Thank Him for what? What have I got to be thankful for?*

Suddenly he was seized with an urge to pray. *But what can I say? Dear God, I have been a bad boy. Please forgive me. Amen.* He snorted. *That was stupid. What had that prayer been, the one Mom had taught him back when he'd been a little boy? Back when—* The unvoiced memory forced itself into his mind. *Back when he was little, and Mom and Dad were happy, and he had a home and—and—No!* Johnny sat up sharply. He didn't even want to think about that.

But it was too late. In a moment the whole flood of old memories swept over him. *Sunday mornings when Dad had read the funnies to him. The days when they'd gone to the lake fishing. The way Mom and Dad used to tease him, laughing and joking. The fun they had. And the night he had first*

*been awakened by their arguing, and how he had
lain there in the dark listening to them yell at each
other. And the other nights. And then the visit to
stay with some "nice people for a few days." That*
had been five years ago, and more.

He buried his head under his arms. He didn't
want the jailer to hear him crying. Finally he fell
asleep, and woke to find it dark. A cold supper lay
on the table. He ate it slowly, then fell back into
a restless sleep.

Breakfast the next morning turned out to be a
roll and a glass of milk. He gobbled it down and
had just managed to fall asleep again when the
clatter of feet and the babble of voices woke him.
He sat up just in time to see Pete being led down
the corridor, hands cuffed in front of him. A policeman was on one side, and a man in a brown suit
walked behind.

"There he is! That yellow little rat!"

Johnny stared at Pete, then realized that Pete
was shouting at him. He turned and stared at the
wall.

"You rat! You cheese rat! Little snitch! I'll
get you! You come to Laffie, and I'll—"

"Shut up!" The man in the suit clapped a hand
over Pete's mouth and hustled him down the hall.
Just as they got by, Johnny heard Pete yell one last
time. "I'll get you—SNITCH" followed by the
whack! of someone getting hit, and then silence.

*So, a rat. A cheese rat, fink, snitch. Was that
him? Well, what if it was? What did it matter what
Pete thought ... what anyone thought? Who cared?*

It didn't matter. Nothing did anymore, did it?

He got up and began walking furiously around the room, swinging his arms from side to side. He wanted to hit something, break something, kick something—anything! He felt all knotted up inside, mad and scared. More than anything else, he was mad! But he didn't know why, or at whom!

Finally he sat down again, picking up the Bible from the spot under the table where he'd thrown it the night before. *Dear God! Dear God!* He wanted to pray. He was scared! But he didn't know what to say. *Dear God ... I ... I know you're real. You've got to be! Help me! Why can't I be like other kids? That's all I want ... a home ... like other kids ... please ... PLEASE!*

The Bible fell open and he saw his name and began reading. "In the beginning was the Word...." He didn't understand, but he kept reading as though his life depended on it. *Please!*

Afternoon brought a visitor. Just after lunch, when the jailer came for his tray, he opened the door and announced: "Lady to see you, son."

"Miss Parsons."

"She give her name, but that weren't it. I forget. From the agency, though. Maybe get you out of here today. You go down to that room there." He pointed toward the far end of the hall.

Johnny looked down at his stockinged feet.

"You won't need shoes. You ain't goin' no place yet."

Johnny shrugged and padded down to the room. It was small, lit by a single bulb, and the only furniture was a steel table and two battered chairs. A woman he'd never met before stood up and smiled at him, holding out her hand. "You must be Johnny Nolan. I'm Miss Crenshaw, your new caseworker."

Johnny took her hand. "What—what happened to Miss Parsons?"

"Sit down." She took a seat and waited for him to say something. Johnny decided that he liked her. She was small, wearing a dark blue suit with a pink rose in the lapel. And she was young. She looked almost as young as his mother, though her blond hair was streaked with gray. And she had smiled and called him "Johnny"—something Miss Parsons had never done in five years.

"The agency felt—thought—uh, decided that it would be best after what happened that—uh, Miss Parsons should let me take over your case," Miss Crenshaw said, and Johnny was surprised and pleased when she let it go at that. He knew that Miss Parsons wouldn't have.

"I'm glad," Johnny said. "I never liked her anyway."

"We thought as much," Miss Crenshaw said. "I suppose she wasn't an easy woman for you to like. She was a little old-fashioned, I guess." She smiled, as though that was a secret between them, and that was when Johnny knew he was going to like her.

"What happens now?" he said, staring at the floor. "I'll get sent up, huh?"

She laughed softly. "No, Johnny, you're not going to get sent up. That's not what you need. What you need is—"

"I need a home and a mom and a dad," Johnny

said, louder than he meant to. "Is that so awful to want?"

"Johnny . . . Johnny." She shook her head slowly. "We're going to get that home for you, a real home. But in—in the meantime. . . ."

Here it comes now.

"In the meantime you'll have to stay—have to stay—"

"Where?"

"I'll be honest," she said. "You're not a little boy any longer. Pete already told the whole story about your running away. It seems that you wanted to back out, after—after he hit Mr. Olaffson—"

"I'm not like Pete!" Johnny said. "I don't want to be—"

"I know that, Johnny. And because we believe you, you won't be going where Pete went. Instead, you're going to the County Detention Center at Fair Oaks."

"You mean—"

"Cleveland, I think the kids call it," she said. "It used to be Cleveland College Hall, didn't it? Well, you'll be there a while. Not long, I hope."

"Why?"

"Because, Johnny, we just don't know what else to do with you."

"I'll go there and *then* get sent up, huh?"

"Not if we can find a good home for you, and we think we may have one already. And we think you'll be happy and better off in the home we find. But you will go to court."

"Court?"

"You did break some laws, you know. Stole a

car. Hit Mr. Olaffson. Ran away."

"But, Pete did—"

"You were with him," she said. "In the eyes of the law, you're every bit as guilty. But since we know the whole story now, the court will take it into consideration."

"So I go to Cleveland and then to court, huh?"

"It's not the end of the world. You *could* have gone to Lafayette. Would you have liked that better?"

Johnny thought of Pete and his threat rang in his mind. "No, I guess I got off lucky," he said, grinning a little.

She stood up. "I'm going to the Olaffson's to get your things now. I should be back to get you about three. The home is sending down a man to go back with us. You should be there in time for supper."

After she was gone, Johnny sat alone in his cell, thinking. *So he was going to Cleveland—Fair Oaks—whatever you wanted to call it. That made him a JD, didn't it? Sure, it was a juvenile home; so he must be a juvenile delinquent now. But it was better than Lafayette, wasn't it? He'd soon find out.*

7

So You Think You're Tough?

CLEVELAND turned out to be a rambling old Victorian mansion, high on a hill, near a gloomy cemetery. Johnny got there just in time to be late for supper, and was served a special meal in the kitchen. He'd just sat down to eat when a big, nearly bald Negro man in blue denims and white tennis shoes sat down across from him.

"You're Johnny Nolan, aren't you? I'm Mister Phillips." He held out his hand and Johnny shook it nervously, noticing how the whiteness of his nails contrasted with the darkness of his skin. He'd never shaken hands with a colored person before.

"The guys all call me Skipper," he said. "I'm Admiral of the little crew here. Counselor in Jefferson Hall anyway. That's where you'll be bunking."

Johnny nodded, concentrating on his dinner. "Every boy gets a room of his own here at the home," Skipper said. "And he's responsible for that room. You'll find that I run a tight ship. I expect those rooms to be seaworthy at all times. Clean and ship-shape. Someone'll show you how I want beds made."

"I get my own room? I thought that—"

"That we had cells here?" Skipper boomed out in laughter, slapping one wide hand on his leg. Johnny realized that he was even bigger than he had first looked. "No, this isn't a jail." He lowered his voice and brought his eyes down to Johnny's level. "Boys are here till the court decides what's best for them—an institution or back with their parents. If they have any—lots don't."

"Mine are divorced," Johnny said.

"Miss Crenshaw showed me your file," Skipper said. "But you get to see them. Don't feel sorry for yourself. That's one thing we don't like here. A lot of fellows don't have any folks at all. If you want to feel sorry for someone, feel sorry for them."

"I guess you're right," Johnny said sheepishly.

"Aye, aye, mate," Skipper said, breaking into a smile again. "You'll find this an easy place to get along. Just two things we don't tolerate here—stealing and fighting. If anyone here catches a guy steal-ing—well, the guys manage to stop that. And if any-one thinks he's tough, I'm a whole lot tougher."

"Aye, aye," Johnny said, and they both laughed.

After dinner they went to the front office and got his things, a fat suitcase and a battered card-board box. His watercolors and a sketch pad were on top of the box. "You an artist?" Skipper asked.

"A little." Johnny took the box while Skipper tucked the suitcase under one arm.

"We've got a Hobby Room here with some paints and stuff. It's a good way to pass the time. Here we are now."

They came to the end of a passageway and he turned to a big steel door, setting down the suitcase. He opened it with a key, revealing a long hallway flanked by about fifteen rooms on either side. "I'll get you a room in a sec."

Johnny looked down the hall. At the far end he saw what appeared to be a big recreation room, with a bunch of guys milling around in it. He could see a couple kids playing pool, and hear the clatter of a Ping-Pong game.

Skipper waved to a tall, thin, dark-haired boy. "Spider, help me get this new man a room."

"Aye, aye," Spider said. "Twenty-six is empty now. Eddie DeMarco went out this afternoon."

"Help him get settled in there then. I'll send Peanuts down with some bedding in a minute." He turned to Johnny. "When you get done, come to the Control Room. I've got some forms to fill out."

"What do I call you?" Spider said when Skipper left.

"Huh? Oh, just Johnny. Johnny Nolan."

"I'm Spider. Actually, it's Paul Kramer, but most of the kids in here got nicknames. You'll learn them all. Here's your room." He pushed the door open and flipped on the light.

"Hey, nice!" Johnny said, looking around. It was a good-sized room with a bed, a writing desk and a chair, and a big wardrobe closet in one corner. There was even a bright rag rug on the floor. A barred window over the bed looked out over a basketball court.

"Just like downtown," Spider said. "What you in for?"

"Waitin' for court."

"I mean, what'd you *do*? I kicked in a bunch of grocery stores. I had almost a hundred bucks when they got me." He lowered his voice. "You got any butts?"

Johnny shook his head. "I don't smoke."

"Oh. But what'd you do, anyway?"

"Ran off from a welfare home—on a farm."

"Oh." Spider sounded disappointed.

Johnny couldn't resist the chance. "We cracked the old man over the head, too, me and another kid. Then we grabbed his car, but smashed it up. He went back to Laffie.

"Hey, man," Spider said. "Good show!"

Johnny shrugged. "I got caught."

"Yeah," Spider said. "Me too. Come on now, I'll get you some sheets from Peanuts and show you how to make a bed. Skipper's a real nut about that."

Lights out came at 9:00. By then Johnny had already gotten the feel of the place. It didn't seem *too* bad, but it wasn't a home. Some of the guys, like Spider, seemed all right. But others seemed just like Pete. One, in particular, he knew he wasn't going to like. He was a big fat kid, with a small cross tattooed on his forehead and a blond crew cut, named Alex. "He's the duke in here," Spider whispered when they first came into the Rec Room.

"What's that?"

Spider gave him a curious look. "It means he's got the bully here. If you got something Alex wants, he takes it away from you. Unless you can whip him. Nobody here can."

Johnny nodded. He almost started to ask Spider why someone didn't tell Skipper about it, if it was so bad. But he caught himself in time. He'd learned *that* much, anyway.

He had a hard time remembering who was who at first. There was a Big Ed and a Little Ed, a colored kid named Schoolboy, a little tiny kid they called Peanuts, and an Indian boy everyone called Chief. He looked mean and Johnny decided to stay away from him.

He was just about due to get his turn at the Ping-Pong table when the lights flicked on and off twice. "Lights out, men!" Skipper's big voice boomed out from the glass-walled Control Room.

Everyone turned and headed down the hall for their rooms. The hall lights had already been turned off, and the dim blue night lights were on. Coming by the third room on the right, Johnny heard some muffled sounds coming through the half-opened door. He looked at Spider questioningly.

"Alex is thumpin' heads," Spider whispered. "Whippin' up on some bong who snitched on him."

"Bong?"

"A goofy kid. Don't pay no attention."

Johnny nodded and looked down at the floor. Just then Alex slipped out the door and dashed across the hall, into his own room. On the way, he sneered at Johnny. Behind him, Johnny heard muffled sobs coming from the room.

"Sleep tight, don't let the bedbugs bite," Spider said, turning into his room. "Bed check in three minutes."

Johnny nodded and walked into his own room, flipping out the light. *So this is what it's like*, he thought, undressing for bed. *Alex can have anything he wants 'cause he's the biggest.* Johnny hoped he didn't have anything Alex wanted.

But he did. It happened just after breakfast the next morning. He and Spider had gone into the Sports Room. About a dozen guys were in there, some wrestling, some lifting weights, and some just goofing off. Johnny was standing along one wall minding his own business when Alex came swaggering over, grinning. He stopped right in front of Johnny and stood staring at a point just below his chin. "I like that."

"Huh?" Then Johnny knew what he meant, the chain around his neck with the half-coin on it that Dad had given him.

"Give me that," Alex said, reaching for it.

"No! My dad gave it—" Johnny raised a hand to protect the coin, but Alex chopped his arm away and grabbed the keepsake, pulling on the chain.

"I said I like it," he said, his voice lower now, and a thin smile creasing his fat lips. "You wanta give it to me?"

"No!"

Alex didn't say a word. He just shrugged and turned away. Then, suddenly, he whirled back and chopped a short right into Johnny's belly.

"Uhhh!" Johnny gasped as the wind went out of him. He put up his hands, sliding sideways. But Alex was too strong. He grabbed one wrist and slammed Johnny flat against the wall, while he pumped a pair of hard rights into his chin. "Now give it to me," he said softly.

Johnny nodded, fighting to get his wind back and make his head stop spinning, while Alex began to slip the chain over his head. The room was very still and Johnny sensed a dozen guys watching him, waiting. Then he made his move.

He jerked his head back suddenly, and let the chain snap, coming loose in Alex's hand. Then he dropped to a crouch, butting Alex hard with his head. Alex let out a surprised grunt and fell back.

Johnny knew he wasn't strong enough to whip Alex, but speed might do it. He bounced a couple sharp punches off Alex's nose and tried to close in. But Alex was too strong. Johnny felt a jolting blow take him in the pit of his stomach, and his knees went soft. He saw the world tilt as he fell, then felt a foot explode in his stomach.

A moment later Alex was crouched over him, and Johnny saw blood streaming from his nose. *At least I got him,* he thought dimly. Then he saw a big fist cocked, the ends of the chain dangling from it, and closed his eyes as the fist crashed into his face. "Gotta whip you good now, kid," Alex grunted, drawing back for another smash.

"Cases," someone yelled. "The man's comin'!"

"Here he comes!"

Alex hopped to his feet, assuming a look of innocence. "You—Spider. Make like you're wrestling him," he barked. "Everybody dummy up now!"

And that's just what it looked like a moment later when Skipper poked his head in the door. "Everything shipshape?"

"Aye, aye!"

And that was that. Except that Alex had his chain now. And except that he'd promised, "Wait till tonight, kid. You're gettin' stomped." But at least he'd fought back. This time.

"Yeah, at least you got him a little," Spider said a half hour later over a game of checkers. "But Alex gets his turn now. You're in a world of trouble, pal."

"Jump me," Johnny grunted. "Alex ain't so tough. He's just big—and that doesn't make it right for him to pick on everyone."

Spider took two checkers in a double jump. "Nooo, but what can *you* do about it? He's too big for anyone in here to whip. I fought him too, ya know. That's my belt he's got on."

"King me." Johnny scratched his chin. It still ached. "You fought him, and I fought him. So neither one of us is ascared of him. Right?"

Spider grunted. "And neither one of us can whip him, either."

"Not alone we can't. But—"

"You ain't thinkin—"

"Well, if both of us was to—"

"Hey, not a bad idea. I'm ready, if you are."

"Come on!" Johnny pushed the checkers off the board. "Let's go find him now. I want my chain back. Together, we can whip the big slob."

Alex was in his room, sitting on the bed and

fiddling with the chain, when Johnny kicked the door open. "What you want, your tail kicked?" Alex grunted. "Get outta here, punk!"

"That's mine!" Before Alex knew what was happening, Johnny had snatched the chain away from him. "I'm takin' it, you big freak!"

Alex unloaded a string of profanity and came off the bed swinging. His first blow caught Johnny on the ear, then Johnny ducked and butted him in the stomach. "Now, Spider!"

Spider leaped into the room, landing crab-like on Alex's back. Alex tilted back with the sudden weight. "Hey, I-aaghh!"

"I got him!" Spider yelled. "Blast him!"

Johnny straightened up to see Alex bent back, his sight blinded by Spider's arm over his face. Johnny put everything he had into a right hand that lost itself in Alex's belly. Alex bellowed with pain at the kick that followed it. Johnny swung again and again, enjoying his revenge. "Let him go now!"

Spider slipped down and Alex stumbled forward, off balance and gasping from the kick in the stomach. He'd just started to raise a fist when Spider chopped him on the neck. His head bobbed and Johnny laced a solid left to his mouth.

"Hey! What the thunder's goin' on here!"

Johnny felt a huge hand grab his hair and send him spinning into the wall. He saw Spider tumble the other way as big Skipper broke the melee up. "Two on one, huh? Tough guys, huh? You tough, Spider?" He grabbed him and slapped his mouth.

Spider burst into tears. "No! It—it was his idea. Johnny told me to. Johnny, he—"

Johnny was on his feet then. "You dirty snitch, Spider!" he yelled. "You dirty cheese rat! Fink!"

Skipper whirled on him. "So you think you're a tough guy, huh? I guess you need the paddle!"

"I—I—" Johnny realized that Alex was watching him, testing him. It gave him a shaky feeling in his stomach, but he looked up at Skipper's big dark face and sneered. "Do what you want to. Get your paddle! I can take it, even if that rat Spider can't!"

Spider watched him with tear-filled eyes. "You— you're a dirty rat yourself, Nolan. A dirty rat!"

Johnny shrugged and let Skipper lead him out for his punishment. *Yeah, I am a dirty rat. I sure am. But I'm getting to be a smarter rat every day.*

Alex didn't say much, just winked at him when he came out of Skip's office a few minutes later rubbing his behind. "I guess you're okay, kid," he said. "Anyone give you any trouble now, you tell 'em to come and see me. Come on now, I'll shoot you some pool. Nine ball, Friday pie on the five, Sunday ice cream on the nine. Okay?"

"Yeah, man," Johnny said.

And that was that. Except that Spider didn't talk to him anymore.

And he had his chain back that night. He found himself lying in bed, twirling it, and staring at the wall when he should have been sleeping. What a louse he was. It made him squirm just to think about what Dad would say if he knew about it.

He threw the chain in the corner and slammed the pillow over his head. Then he got up, retrieved the chain, and tied the ends together. An hour later, when he finally fell asleep, he had it on.

8

You're a Jailbird Like Your Father

THE NEXT DAY he felt even worse about it, and he went out of his way to get a chance to talk to Spider alone. He waited until he spotted him in the Hobby Room working on a Spitfire model, and walked in. "Hi," he said, trying to smile.

No answer.

"I'm—I'm sorry, I guess," Johnny said. "I mean—"

"Alex know you're here?" Spider said, not looking up. "You're *his* pal now. He wouldn't want you rapping to a rat like me."

"I said I was sorry," Johnny said weakly.

"So you're sorry. All right." Spider turned back to his work. Johnny stood there a minute, then turned and slowly walked back into the Rec Room. Alex was goofing around the pool table.

"Wanta shoot a game of rotation?"

Johnny shrugged. "I'm gonna go lay down."

"I owe you my Friday pie. Let's play for it."

"No. Not now," Johnny said. "Later on."

Alex was standing in front of him now. "Win and quit, huh? I *said* I wanta play pool. Now!" He pushed Johnny, just a little.

"I don't wanta play now." Johnny pushed him back, just a little more. "And I ain't gonna."

"You gettin' bad with me now? I thought we was gonna be tight, man. Don't get bad now." He made a grab to snatch up Johnny's shirt front.

Johnny pushed his hand away. "Lay off, Alex. I don't wanta play pool, and you can't make me." He pushed him again.

"All right, tough guy, break it up!" Skipper stepped up suddenly and pushed them apart. He looked at Johnny and shook his head. "You always in trouble or something?"

Johnny stared at the floor sullenly.

"Ain't talkin', huh? You better go think about things a while. You got forty-eight in your room."

As Johnny turned, he saw Spider standing in the doorway of the Hobby Room. He caught his eye and winked at him. Spider grinned and winked back. *Even Steven.* So maybe a couple days restricted to his room might not be so bad at that. Now he could get a chance to draw some pictures. And think.

But he found he'd rather draw, and not think about things at all.

Wednesday brought a visitor. He'd finished the 48-hour restrictions after breakfast, but he'd stayed in his room anyway, trying to get a picture done. It was getting worse with each attempt, and he was out of six colors, and almost out of three more, and needed a new 00 brush to boot.

Skipper poked his head in the door. "Your case-worker wants to see you. That big room on the left, by the main door."

"Maybe she knows when I'm gettin' out of here."

"Maybe," Skipper said. His face said: *I sure hope so.*

"When are you getting out of here, Johnny?" Miss Crenshaw said. "Next week for sure. Monday, in fact."

"Honest?"

She nodded. "You'll go to court Monday morning. And we've got a home for you. A wonderful family named Knowles. A week from today, you should be settled with them."

"Where do they live?"

"Just south of the city, not far from Minnetonka. In Birchdale. Actually, it's just north of Birchdale. There's a school six blocks away, and a big park just a block away. I think this is finally going to be the home you've always wanted, Johnny."

"Boy! Will I be glad to get out of here!"

"You don't like it, huh? How have you been getting along here, Johnny?"

He shrugged. "Not so hot. I just got off restrictions this morning. That means I—"

"I know. Mr. Phillips told me."

"Well, if you talked to him, why'd you ask me?"

"To see what you'd say."

"You thought you could catch me in a lie, huh?" He crossed his arms and turned to stare out the window. "Well, maybe I did have some trouble, but Skipper don't know the whole story!"

"I know that," Miss Crenshaw said softly. "Things often look different from the other side of the fence. That's why I asked you. I want to hear your side of it."

Johnny told her, and by the time he was done they were both shaking their heads and grinning. "I guess I did the wrong thing at first," Johnny said. "And then I tried to do the right one and still got in trouble."

"Life's like that. And—oh, I brought you a present." She pointed to a bag on the table. "From your father."

"From Dad! Did you see him?"

"I just came from—" she stopped, putting a hand to her mouth, then shook her head. "Well—you know about your father, I guess. I mean, you know about his—his sickness—"

"He drinks too much," Johnny said in a low voice. "But only 'cause his back hurts—where he got shot in Korea. He wouldn't drink at all if it didn't hurt him so bad. That's why he drinks." He knew it was a lie, but she didn't argue over the point the way he knew Miss Parsons would have.

Miss Crenshaw nodded. "He's in the hospital, over at the Veterans Hospital in St. Paul."

Johnny leaned forward. "Is—is he—real sick?"

"No, he's just—" Her voice was low too. "Drinking. But he's getting better every day. He should be out tomorrow."

"Whew! You sure he'll be okay?"

"Yes. He's in good care, Johnny. But don't you want to see your present? He gave me some money and asked me to pick it out. I did the best I could, but I've never done any painting."

He snatched up the bag and spilled the contents on the table. "An oil set, and canvases, and brushes! A real oil set!" Impulsively he hugged Miss Crenshaw and kissed her on the cheek, something he'd have never dreamed of doing with Miss Parsons.

"I'm glad you like it," she said, flushing a little. "Your dad said you would."

"Boy! Now I've got something to do while I wait for court! This will really make the time fly!"

"Paintin', huh?" Spider said an hour later, poking his head into Johnnys' room.

"Tryin' to. My dad sent these to me. Nice, huh?"

Spider inspected the maple box, the shiny tubes, the sparkling white canvases. "Pretty fair."

"I want to do a picture for my mom. She oughta be here to visit me this Sunday. My caseworker said she called and said she would. But I don't have anything to copy."

"You mean like a landscape? Trees and an old barn or something?" Spider said. "Like that?"

"Yeah, you—"

Spider snapped his fingers. "Hold the fort." He turned and dashed from the room. A minute later he was back, a tattered *Life* magazine in hand. "I think I saw—here!" He flipped the magazine to Johnny. "How's that?"

Johnny looked at the picture. It was a full page, in color, of a New England autumn scene. "Just what I wanted! Thanks, pal."

"Can—can I watch you?" Spider said. "I mean, it won't bother you—"

"No, if you don't get bored."

"I won't."

But an hour later, Johnny was alone. Spider did get bored. Johnny was so absorbed that he never noticed his leaving until after he was gone. But by then he was so busy painting that he didn't care.

The rest of the week raced by. Johnny stayed in his room, painting, painting, painting. Twice he almost had the picture finished and then decided it *still* wasn't right and started on a fresh canvas.

Saturday morning he finally got the big blocks of color in just the way he wanted them. The sky was the top third of the canvas, indicated now by a thin wash of cerulean blue. That gave a sense of depth against the rough sweeps of magenta, which were eventually meant to be hills. And the dark ochers and umbers in the foregrounds made a foundation on which to swirl in the hundred gay shades of a forest in autumn.

Johnny spent the whole day in his own little world, lost in his painting. He was trying a method he had never used before. Just a month ago he had read someplace that all good artists painted this way, blocking in their masses in broad washes, and then laying on colors, building from the deepest shadows to the most brilliant highlights. That way, the whole picture was in the same state of completion at any time. Before, he'd always found himself painting in the details on a house before he'd even started laying down a base color for the sky behind it.

The new method worked so well that he just sat and stared in happiness at the painting when it was done late Saturday evening. He set it on the chair and stood back, proud of himself.

"Say, you *can* paint, Johnny. Good work, mate."

"Huh?" Johnny looked up to see Skipper poking his head in the door. "Oh, you scared me. I was so wrapped up—"

"I know," Skipper said. "It's nearly eleven o'clock." He glanced at his watch. "Ten to."

Johnny gave him a puzzled look. "But, lights out is at—"

"I left your light on. You seemed so busy when I peeked in a few hours ago, I thought I'd better let you finish. Spider said you wanted to have it ready for your mom tomorrow. Is it all done now?"

"Yeah, and thanks," Johnny said. "Just gotta sign it. Here." He took a #0 brush, dipped it in raw sienna, and added a drop of linseed oil. Then in the lower corner he signed in block letters *J. Nolan, 6-20-66-Fair Oaks.* "Just like the pros, huh?"

"You bet," Skipper said with a grin. "Now, you better get some sleep, mate."

"Aye, aye," Johnny said with a short laugh. "And—and you know what, Skipper?" He scuffed a toe on the floor. "You—you're a pretty good guy. You're okay."

Johnny hadn't known a colored man could blush, but Skipper did. "You get to sleepin," he said in a husky voice, backing out the door.

Johnny lay there in the dark a long while, staring at the wall, trying to sort and untangle the events of the week. He knew they meant something, formed a pattern or something, but he just couldn't put them together. He had a vague feeling they were all going to add up to something good. He thought of the odd feeling he'd had in jail, when he'd tried to pray. *Well?*

He stared at the ceiling, as if he could see right through it, right through the sky, all the way up to someplace, wherever God was supposed to be. *Maybe*, he thought. "Thanks," he said in a low voice, feeling a little foolish—and a little grateful—all at once. *You heard, I think.*

He rolled over and lay staring at his painting until sleep overtook him. When he finally fell asleep, he was dreaming of what Mom would say when she saw it tomorrow.

"This is a fine place to have to come and visit you." Mom looked around the visiting room, fixing her eye on the big window just to the left of the old sofa she shared with Johnny. It was barred, and looked out on a field enclosed with a high wire fence.

"Shucks," Johnny said. "I can't help it."

"I don't know why I came to see you. I want you to know that I'm ashamed of you, Johnny. Imagine— what you and that boy did to that old man. And then stealing a car! I never raised you—"

"Mom!" Johnny said. Three or four other kids were getting visits from their families, and they were all looking at her. Johnny had known it would mean trouble as soon as he had seen her walk in. She still had a party dress on and her perfume didn't cover the smell that told him she'd been drinking.

"Well, I can't help that," she said. "I hope you're mighty proud of yourself. Look at you—a jailbird! A fine son!"

Johnny shrugged and stared at his feet.

"I'm not surprised, though," she said, her voice rising to a familiar shrill note. "I should have known what to expect. Like father, like son, they say—"

"Don't you say that!" He glared at her, staring with cold fury.

"Look who's getting touchy," she said. "My fine young jailbird son. Just like your father! He was—"

"Don't you talk about him! He loves me more than you ever did. He's the one—"

Her voice broke in over his. "Johnny, it's time you grew up and faced the facts of life. He's no good. Your father is just a no-good drunk. And you're starting out to be just like—"

"NO HE AIN'T!" His fists balled in anger and tears streamed down his face.

"Your father is a no-good drunk," she said in a cold, flat voice. "And you're starting out like him —a jailbird. You're not even thirteen. Johnny—"

"SHUT UP! I hate you!" He broke into sobs and raced halfway across the room. "I hate you!" he yelled. "I don't care if you ever see me again! I hate you!"

He turned and raced down the corridor for Jefferson Hall, and down the hall, and into his room. He slammed the door shut behind him and jammed the chair under the knob.

That was when he remembered the painting. The painting he had done just for her. He plucked it off the window ledge, and felt the half-dry paint smear under his thumb. Tears streaming down his face, he tried to rip it in half.

But it was too heavy; so he bent it double, and stamped on it. Then he ripped it, and bent it, and ripped it, crying and tearing and talking to himself all at once. "I hate you! My dad ain't what you say! I hate you! I hate you!"

Then he flung himself on the bed and cried until nothing was left but a dull ache in his heart that would never quite go away.

9

This Is Your Home Now, Johnny

THE next morning, when Skipper stood by the big steel hall door with the court list in his hand, Johnny was ready and waiting. He'd put on his best pair of cords, the nearest thing he had to a dress shirt, and for once his hair wasn't hanging down in his eyes. He ran into Spider when he came out of his room.

"Good luck, pal. Hope you get a good one."

Johnny winked, feeling suddenly exuberant. "I'm halfway out the door already."

"Be careful what you say to the judge," Spider said. "That's important. You oughta get Darby, and he's a cranky old coot."

"I'll say what he wants to hear," Johnny said.

"All right—Court Call. Line it up!" Skipper bellowed. "Come on, Nolan. Waitin' on ya!"

Four other boys were going to court that morning. The five of them and Skipper made the long walk to the court chambers in silence, each lost in his own thoughts. The courtroom turned out to be big and solemn-looking. Everything seemed to be made with polished oak and the whole room seemed full of hushed expectations. Thirty or more people sat scattered among the benches in the back. Johnny brightened a little when he saw Miss Crenshaw, a red rose in her hair, waving to him.

He looked up at Skipper. "Can I—"

"Go ahead now, boy. And—" He paused and patted him on the shoulder. "And good luck now."

He slipped into the seat next to Miss Crenshaw, looking about him in the vague hope that Dad might be here. He knew better than to expect his mother, after what had happened yesterday. It would be at least a week before she wrote him a long, weepy "I'm sorry" letter—the kind she always did. *But Dad—*

"Your dad called yesterday. He got out of the hospital on Saturday," Miss Crenshaw said. "He said he didn't think he should come after all. He—"

"I understand," Johnny said. "I know how he—" He shrugged and she didn't say anything for a moment. Then she leaned over and said. "The Knowles are in the chambers with Judge Darby now."

"The Knowles. You mean—"

"Yes. You should be on the way home with them in an hour or so. How does that sound?"·

"Great! What—what are they—well, what are they like, you know?"

"You'll see." Just then the door at the far end of the courtroom, to one side of the judge's bench, opened. A man in a dark suit leaned out and beckoned to them. "They want us in chambers now."

"In the chamber?"

She nodded, getting to her feet. "We'll just all get together in the judge's chambers and talk things over. Then Judge Darby will decide whether you go home with the Knowles or stay here."

"Or go to Lafayette?" Johnny said, following her through the narrow aisle.

"I wouldn't worry about that."

The first thing Johnny saw in the slightly darkened room was Judge Darby, sitting behind a sheaf of papers at his desk. He was tall and dignified, very old, with gold-framed glasses and a shock of yellow-white hair that stood out in bright relief against the walnut paneling on the walls.

"Sit down there." Johnny did as the bailiff directed and sank into a huge green leather chair directly in front of the desk. Miss Crenshaw sat on a sofa along one wall next to a man and woman who, Johnny decided, must be the Knowles.

The judge remained silent, rummaging through the papers, and Johnny took opportunity of the pause to sneak a look over at the Knowles. Mr. Knowles appeared to be in his forties, big and trim in an athletic way, with a close cut shock of iron-gray hair. He had friendly blue eyes and a smile on his tanned face. Next to him sat Mrs. Knowles, as short as he was tall, dark and pretty, with glossy black hair. She seemed plump and pleasant. Johnny decided they were nice people and hoped he was right.

92

The bailiff spoke to the judge in a whisper. The judge tilted his head back and stared out over the pile of papers at Johnny. "So you're the Nolan boy, eh? Well, what do you have to say for yourself?"

Johnny didn't know what to say. *Maybe he's testing me,* he thought. But he couldn't think of anything to say.

"Proud to be here? Like it behind bars, do you?"

Johnny shook his head vigorously. "No! I'm not proud, and I sure don't like it here."

The old judge nodded. "Hmm. Got yourself in a little scrape, though. I hope you've had enough of places like this. There are a lot worse ones, you know."

Johnny nodded and the judge went right on talking.

"Well, lad, you're one of the lucky ones. These good people here said they want to take you along and give you a decent home—the kind a boy needs. I think they can, and I'm gonna say yes. Think you can stay put this time?"

Johnny nodded and stared nervously at the Knowles. "Yes, I'm sure I—"

"The court is going to make sure that you stay in line. We are putting you on probation. And this gentleman here"—he poked to his left with his thumb, and Johnny saw a man he hadn't even known was in the room before, sitting in a wooden chair and thumbing through a thick file folder—"is going to see that you obey the probation rules. This is Mr. Fitzpatrick, your new probation officer. Shake the man's hand, son."

Mr. Fitzpatrick stood up, and seemed to just

get bigger and bigger. Johnny stared up at him. He was red-haired and freckled, and as big as he could be. He looked like a football player.

"Well, Johnny, we're going to see a lot of each other; so we might as well start off as friends." His voice was light and had a touch of a laugh in it, surprising in a man his size. And the hand he offered smothered Johnny's.

A few minutes later introductions had been made all around. Judge Darby stood up and, as if on signal, everyone prepared to leave. "You come with me now," Fitzpatrick said. "We've got a few rules to explain and papers to fill out. The Knowles will wait out front for you." And that was the end of court.

A half hour later Johnny went back to Jefferson Hall, whistling and skipping. Nothing now but to get his things and go. Things had turned out just super! When he'd gone down to the probation office with Mr. Fitzpatrick, Johnny had learned that not only did he look like a football player, but, until two years ago, he had been one—a tackle with the Vikings.

"I was raised in a place like this," Fitzpatrick said, his eyes looking at Johnny as though he saw himself sitting there. "Orphanage in Colorado. So I quit playin' games and decided to work at keepin' other boys out of these places. That's what probation rules are for."

The rules turned out to be simple. Mainly, it was just a matter of staying out of trouble, obeying the Knowles, and taking the bus down to the state office building once a week on Tuesday afternoons to report to Mr. Fitzpatrick. He gave Johnny a card with his address and phone number on it. The name was crossed out and in its place was a penciled "Red." "Anytime you got a problem, just call for Red," he said, laughter slipping into his voice. "I'm Red to all my boys and we all share our problems. Got that?"

"Got it!" Johnny said, deciding that he was going to like Red. It didn't look as though probation under him was going to be half as bad as some of the guys in Cleveland—like Alex—said it was.

And he got a chance to talk with Miss Crenshaw on his way back from the office to Jefferson Hall. "I'm glad things have gone so well, Johnny," she said. "You know, I won't be seeing too much of you now. Officially, you're in the custody of the court now. But—but I will stop in to see you when I can. I've known you only a short while, but—"

"I'm gonna miss you," Johnny said impulsively. And it was true. In hardly more than a week he had grown to like her better than he had liked Miss Parsons in five years. "I hope I get to see you a—a lot!"

"Thank you, Johnny. That's—that's very nice," she said quickly, then walked away, dabbing at something on her cheek with a tiny pink hanky.

Yup, things had turned out just super!

Whistling, Johnny sauntered into Jefferson Hall.

"Hey! You made it huh?"

"Huh?" Johnny looked up to see that he'd walked right by Spider without seeing him. "Yeah! Just got to get my things packed up now— and go!"

"All packed," Spider said. "I did it for you when the call came down. Skipper's got your stuff in the office now, waiting."

Johnny hesitated, then stuck out his hand.

"Where you goin' to?" Spider asked.

"Foster home out in Birchdale. Near the lake, I guess."

"Honest? I might wind up out there too. Nearby, anyway."

"You?"

Spider nodded vigorously. "Sure. I got an aunt and uncle who live out there. My agent's been tryin' to get them to take me for a month. If they do, then—"

"That'd be swell," Johnny said. "I mean, wouldn't either of us know anybody out there and—" His voice trailed off. *Did he really want a reminder of this place showing up?* He forced a grin. "Well, take it easy now. I better get hustlin'."

Five minutes later he was walking out of Cleveland for good. He looked back just for a moment, frowned, then got in the car with the Knowles.

They drove a block in uncomfortable silence, then Mr. Knowles broke the ice. "Well, Johnny," he said, smiling a little, "I suppose you're wondering what to call us. I'm Smiley and this is Ma."

"Smiley?"

"He picked it up when he was a ballplayer," Ma said. "And Ma is just—just Ma. When I scold you, though, you better call me Mom." She smiled to let him know that she wasn't the scolding kind.

"Were you a ballplayer?" Johnny asked. "I mean *really*?"

Smiley nodded. "I caught for a couple years in the minors. For the old Indianapolis club. Till I met Ma, anyway. Our boy Ricky is quite a ballplayer, too. We better tell him about the kids, Mother."

"We've got three," she said. "Ricky, he's our boy. And he's what—nineteen now, dear?"

"He'll be twenty come Christmas," Smiley said.

"And then we have little Tom, our Indian boy. We call him Tom-Tom. He's full-blooded Chippewa."

"And five years of real boy," Smiley added with a grin.

"And Nancy is six now."

"Three kids, huh?" Johnny said.

"Well, Ricky is ours," Ma said. "And Tom-Tom and Nancy and now you—three we've made ours. So we've got four in all now. And you're going to be a big brother. Have you ever been a big brother?"

Johnny shook his head. "No—but it sounds like fun!"

The house turned out to be a big brick one, sitting by itself in the middle of the block with vacant lots on both sides. "I like a lot of room," Smiley said, turning into a long gravel drive that led to a double garage with an upstairs on it. It had once been a small house itself. The yard behind the house was walled in with a redwood fence and was at least as big as a football field. "Come on. I'll show you the south forty," Smiley said, braking to a stop in front of the garage.

Just then a tall, blond-haired boy in Levi's and a green baseball cap came trotting around the side of the garage, followed by a chubby little Indian boy dragging a baseball bat.

"This is Ricky," Smiley said, introducing them. "And this is Tom-Tom."

"Welcome home, Johnny," Ricky said, shaking his hand. "I was just giving Tom-Tom here some batting tips."

Tom-Tom grinned up at Smiley. "An' I hit a good'n too. It went a mile, I betch! Almost." His dark eyes darted to Johnny, open and friendly. "Your name Johnny? You come to live here too, huh? You can play ball with me, huh? Huh, Smiley? Yes?"

"Yup!" Johnny said, almost breaking into laughter at Tom-Tom's excited rush of words. Being a big brother already seemed like fun!

"He'll run you ragged," Ricky said. "He's one hundred percent pure energy."

"Ricky can put your stuff in the house," Ma said, coming around the car. "I think Smiley wants to show off the yard to you. Where's—"

"Nancy?" Ricky finished. "Out by the swimming pool reading."

"She wouldn't play with us!" Tom-Tom said, stamping a foot. "She says Tom-Tom plays too mean! Huh, Ricky?"

Smiley mussed his hair. "Well, she's only a little girl and you're a big boy, huh?"

" 'N strong!" Tom-Tom said. "I help Ricky, Huh? I can come 'n play with Johnny then too, huh, Johnny?"

"In a little while, pal," Smiley said. He pushed open the gate to the yard. "Come on, son, I'll show you our yard."

The yard really was worth a trip. At the far end was a home plate, a chicken wire backstop, a first base, and a pitcher's mound. "I tried to make it as real as possible for Ricky," Smiley explained. "He's got two years left at college and then he's got a minor league contract if he wants it—as a pitcher."

"Is he playin' now?" Johnny asked.

"No, he's spending the summer as a counselor at Camp Kitchegummee. But he took a few days off so he could meet you. He goes back tomorrow. But he plans to come back weekends for a while till you get settled here. And, anyway, he's managed the Park League team over at Longfellow Park for three summers, and he likes to check on them too."

"He sounds like quite a ballplayer," Johnny said.

"He's quite a boy, Ricky is," Smiley said proudly. He walked on in silence a moment. "And this is our swimming pool, if we ever get it dug. I've been digging it off and on for two years. Right now it's just a big hole."

Johnny stared at the hole in front of him. A little more work and it would be a fine pool. "I can shovel," he said.

Smiley winked. "That's the spirit. Oh, there's Nancy. See?" He pointed with his thumb over to a screened-in little garden shack covered with ivy vines. "She's very shy. There. See her?"

Johnny stared hard and then saw a head of red hair and a freckled face staring out at them through the screening. "She looks afraid," he said, looking up at Smiley curiously.

"Nancy was very shy when she first came here,"

Smiley said. "Her mother was very mean to her and—the court gave her to us. She needs a lot of affection. She needs to learn to know she is loved, and she needs a big brother to love." He gave Johnny a deep look. "You'll have responsiblity here," he said. "And love. This is your home now, Johnny."

This is your home now, Johnny. Smiley's words were still echoing in his ears hours later when Ma came in, kissed him good-night, and flicked off the light in his room. *His* room—*his* home—*his* family! He felt so full of happiness and excitement that sleep was a long time coming. Everything was turning out so nice. Tom-Tom had taken to him like a puppy and Nancy, though she had run and hid when he tried to talk to her, had come tiptoeing back to watch him playing catch with Ricky.

And Ricky was everything Johnny had ever dreamed of in a big brother. He was a big kid, but he didn't treat Johnny like a little kid. Maybe that was what he liked so much about the place. At supper, when Smiley had started to say grace and Johnny was taken by surprise, he liked the way Ricky had said, "God gives us everything, Johnny. It's only right to thank Him." And that had been all.

Or he liked the way Smiley had written his name down on the chore chart with dates and check marks. "Everyone here has chores to do. You'll have certain times to carry out garbage, and wipe dishes, and sweep the porch. You'll get an allowance, and you'll have responsibility. Everyone here has a part in this family. Even Nancy has chores to do, and little Tom-Tom, and now you, because this is your home now, Johnny."

10

Can You Play Third Base?

THREE DAYS flew by so rapidly that Johnny hardly noticed them passing. Half the reason was Tom-Tom. He really *did* run him ragged. First he wanted to play catch, and then tag, and then hide-and-seek. And then he happened to come upstairs and catch Johnny, sitting in his room, sketching a view out the window in watercolors. "Paint Tom-Tom a picture! Paint me a picture, Johnny!" he had shouted, bursting into the room.

"Sure, what do you want?" Johnny asked. Tom-Tom frowned at the floor a minute, then began jumping up and down. "An Injun! Paint Tom-Tom an Injun. Please, Johnny! Paint Tom-Tom an Injun!"

Johnny shook his head. "I—I don't think I can."

Tom-Tom shook his head back and forth wildly and yanked off his T-shirt. "No, no! Paint *Tom-Tom* Injun. Me, Johnny!"

"Huh?" Then he understood. "No, Tom-Tom. I can't do that. Ma'll get mad and—"

"Puuull-leeze!" Tom-Tom said, making an awful frown.

Johnny looked at his paint box. Well, it was only watercolors, and they would wash right off, and Tom-Tom would cry or something if he didn't. "Okay," he said, shaking his head in defeat. "But then you have to go and wash it right off." He dipped into his box and squeezed dabs of magenta, viridian, cobalt blue, chrome yellow, and manganese violet on his tin mixing tray. "First a dot here." And he put a yellow spot on the end of his nose. "And some violet stripes now—zoop! zoop!" He brushed a pair of thick violet stripes down Tom-Tom's chest, and Tom-Tom giggled. "It's cold, Johnny!"

A moment later, Tom-Tom stood there almost shaking with excitement—a red arrow danced on his forehead, blue zig zags wif-waffled down his cheeks, a row of green polka dots adorned his chin, and his eyes were ringed in yellow.

"There! Now, go and look at your—" He heard muffled giggling and looked up to see Nancy peeking in at them, leaning around the doorway. "Hi!" he said. "Come on in and look at big chief Tom-Tom."

She nodded her head shyly and took a hesitant step into the room, never taking her eyes from Johnny. He sat there quietly, not wishing to frighten her, and even Tom-Tom seemed to grow still for the moment. "Can—can I," she whispered softly, pointing at the brush on the mixing pan.

Johnny nodded, dipped it in blue, and handed it to her. Her face looking very solemn, she reached out, standing on tiptoe, and streaked a wavy blue line down Tom-Tom's chest. Then she put the brush down and said softly, "Thank you, Johnny."

Just then Tom-Tom leaped up and came down with a shrill "Woo-woo-woo!" Nancy shrieked in mock fright and raced for the door. Tom-Tom danced about the room, clapping his hand over his mouth and yowling, "Wooo-wooo-woooo" at the top of his lungs.

"Tom-Tom!" Johnny shouted "Quiet! Do you want—"

"What on earth? I declare I never—"

He looked up and saw Ma standing in the doorway, Nancy peering out from behind her skirts. Ma stood there, hands on hips staring while Tom-Tom stopped in mid-leap, one foot in the air, his hand over his mouth. Johnny just waited for the explosion.

And Ma burst out into rollicking laughter. "My two little boys," she chuckled, coming over and hugging both of them to her. "If this isn't the funniest thing I've seen in a month of Sundays," she wheezed. "Tom-Tom, you little imp! And you're another, Johnny. Land sakes! I just wish I had a camera!"

Johnny felt a tiny hand clutching his and looked down to see Nancy smiling up at him, her blue eyes open very wide and a trace of a smile on her face. "I like you," she said softly.

The next day he spent the whole morning teaching her how to use watercolors. And he was surprised at how hard she tried. He'd never in his

whole life met a little girl who seemed so grave and solemn. She hardly ever seemed to smile. But she smiled for him when he told her how much he liked her painting of a cow—even though it looked more like a green horse than anything he could think of.

"You think it's a pretty cow?" she said. "Honest, Johnny?"

"It's the prettiest cow I ever saw," he said gravely. "You like to paint, don't you?"

"I wanna paint some more, too. A secret picture, can I? I'll be real careful and—"

"A secret?" Johnny tickled her under the chin. "What kind of a secret, Missy Button-nose?"

"A *secret* secret!" she said, giggling. "Can I? Please?"

"Go ahead."

Ma poked her head in the door and motioned for him to come over. They both stood there for a moment watching Nancy mixing paints, lost to the world. Then he followed Ma into the kitchen. "She really takes to you," she said. "I'm glad of that, Johnny. She really opens up to you. She's never done that before."

Johnny felt a blush spreading over his face. "Aww, I just—"

She rubbed a hand through his hair. "And now you've got a little brother that needs you. Tom-Tom's out back pouting and crying about something. I guess he had a scrape with the Winslow kids down the block. He wants to come and cry to me, but he thinks that's for little kids. You go see him."

Tom-Tom was sitting behind the garage, his feet dug into holes in the soft dirt, sniffing and crying. He looked up and glared when Johnny came shuffling around the garage. "Go away!" he shouted. "Go 'way, Johnny!"

Johnny sat down next to him. "Trouble, pal?"

Tom-Tom sat in stony silence for a moment, then broke into sobs and put his head on Johnny's shoulder. "They chased me away, Johnny. They hit me and told me to go home!" He rubbed a grimy fist

106

in his eyes. "They said they don't want to play with no ol' Injun. How come they called me ol' Injun and made me go home, Johnny? They told Tom-Tom, 'Go 'way, Injun boy.' How come, Johnny?"

Johnny stared at his feet. "Well, pal," he said slowly, "I guess maybe they wish they were like you too, but they can't be. And so they get mad and treat you mean. They wish they could be *real* Indians instead of just having to pretend they are."

"You think so, huh? Honest?" Tom-Tom sat up, grinning.

"Sure," Johnny said. "Look at—at Sitting Bull and Tonto and all kinds of famous Indians. When they play Indians, they can only pretend, but you don't have to."

"Tom-Tom *real* Indian," Tom-Tom said loudly, jumping up and grinning. "Ugh! You play-um catch with Chief Tom-Tom."

"Ugh!" Johnny said. "Me play Chief Muddy Face!"

They both broke into laughter. Then Tom-Tom showed Johnny the box in the garage where Smiley kept all the baseball stuff.

Johnny was surprised at how well Tom-Tom caught for such a little kid. "Throw 'em high!" he begged. And Johnny arched a high blooper. Tom-Tom caught it neatly and pegged it back. "Higher!" he yelled.

After a little he yelled, "Watch *me* throw." He backed up, took a run with the ball, and threw it with all his might, tumbling head over heels in the act. Johnny was so surprised that he forgot to watch the ball. When he turned around, it was bouncing off the fence. He made a grab for it, but missed.

"It went out in the driveway," he yelled. "I'll get it."

"I got it!"

"Huh?" He looked up to see a boy about his own age, coming through the gate. "Here!" the boy flipped him the ball. "You must be the new kid that came to live with Smiley and them, huh? What's your name?"

"Johnny Nolan."

"I'm Butch Bennet," the boy said. He rubbed a hand across his brown crew-cut and grinned. "Smiley's a great guy, ain't he? And Ma and Ricky too. A couple guys came with me. They're in the house bummin' cookies off Ma. Wanta meet them?"

Fifteen minutes later Johnny found himself on the way to Longfellow Park to play ball with three new friends: Butch, Sam Hill—the tall, red-haired one—and Toughie—the short, freckle-faced one. "We just got a pickup game," Butch said. "A bunch of kids from Morningside wanta play some nine-man softball, and—"

"And we need someone to fill in at third base," Toughie Morrison finished. "I can't 'cause I'm the manager. Ricky was the manager before, but he's working at that camp now and—"

"And we're hoping you can play third base for us," Butch said.

"Yeah, can you play third base?" Sam asked.

Johnny looked around. "Well, to be honest, I'm not much good. I never played much, and—"

"I didn't ask you if you were Clete Boyer," Toughie said with a grin. "This is just an ol' pickup softball game. Wanta try?"

"I'll try," Johnny said. "But—"

"It's just for fun anyway," Sam said. "Here come a couple of the gang now." He pointed to a bike coming down the street. A big kid with thick glasses was bucking a little blond-haired guy on the bars. "That's Goggles," Sam said. "Our left-handed power."

"And the guy on the bars is Teddy Thomas. He plays shortstop. And he ain't really much good. But he tries."

"That's what's important anyway, ya know," Toughie said. "Right?"

Johnny grinned. "Right."

The game turned into a disaster, but Johnny had fun. He handled his first two chances well enough. But then, in the second inning, he came in to take a hard grounder on the short hop and it turned into a tough chance ball that walked right up his arm, bouncing off his nose and going down the third base line for extra bases. He sat up, rubbing the pain from his cheek, while jeers and cheers went up from the guys. Sam came walking over from the mound. "You get hurt?"

Johnny got up, shaking his head a little. "My fault," he said, a blush spreading over his face. "I shoulda had that."

"Baloney," Sam said. "That happens to anyone. Good try."

"Nice try, Johnny," Toughie hollered in from the

third base coaching box. "Don't let it shake you."

At the plate he did a little better. He lucked into a walk on his first time up, took third on a pair of passed balls, and scored when Goggles lined to deep center.

The next two times up he struck out. But then in the seventh with the bases full, after the Morningside pitcher lost all his control, he got hit on the shoulder with a high tight curve. That forced in the run that proved to be the margin of victory. And he found that his shoulder didn't hurt at all when he realized that.

An hour later he found himself sitting in the shade of the bandstand in the middle of the park, talking over the ball game with his new gang of friends. "You did all right," Goggles said. "We won five-to-four and you scored two runs."

"None of us is anything great," Butch said. "We just play for fun anyway. You wanta be on our regular team, permanent? You know Smiley is our sponsor, don't you?"

"I didn't know that," Johnny said. "And I'm not much good, but if you guys want me, I'll try."

"That's all we want," Sam said.

"At least till we get someone else then," Toughie said. "Shucks, you did okay today."

"Yeah, we gotta get organized pretty soon," Sam said. "The Park Board League starts in a week, and we ain't even got our jerseys yet." He looked at a tall, red-haired kid named Terry. "Didn't your dad—"

"Yeah, he brought a whole boxful of white jerseys from the store—nice ones too. And a box of new baseball caps. But the jerseys are just plain white ones, and—"

"Yeah, we need numbers on them and stuff so we can look sharp, like the other teams."

"Right," Sam said. "We need numbers on them and we oughta have the *Birchdale Indians* on them in red, and a picture of an Indian too."

"How you gonna do that, wise guy?" Toughie said.

"Yeah, got any bright ideas?" Butch said.

"Hey!" Johnny said, sitting up suddenly. "I got an idea!"

Everyone looked at him. "Well, let's have it!" Butch said.

"Well, you got plain white jerseys, right?"

"Right."

"Well, I can draw pretty good, and I think I could make up some stencils, and use textile paint, and put numbers on them, and a nice Indian head. I can even put everybody's name on them, if you want to."

"Hey, can you really do that?" Butch said.

"Great!" Goggles said.

"Sure, I made a lot of tablecloths like that before," Johnny said. "I can make a real good stencil of an Indian head too. It won't cost much. Say, if we each kick in a buck or so—"

Butch dug in his pocket. "I got a buck and a half to start."

"I got a lot of nickels at home in my bank," Toughie added.

"I can get the paint wholesale at my dad's drugstore," Goggles offered.

And just like that it was settled. Johnny was on the team, and Johnny was suddenly an important member of the team. And he had a dozen new friends. He was just bubbling over with good feeling when Butch walked home with him that afternoon.

"You like it out here?" Butch asked.

"Yeah, you bet," Johnny said.

"Smiley's a great guy, isn't he? He's our youth leader at church too. Boy, do we have fun! You gonna come to church Sunday? We got a game this week, but we oughta have a picnic a week from Saturday. We have lots of fun."

"Why, er—yeah, I'll be there," Johnny said.

"Me and Sam'll be over after supper to play a little pepper. I mean, you try, but—"

"I'm no third baseman," Johnny said. "But I'll try."

"We'll help you, and Smiley can too. I wish Ricky was here. Boy, he's a great guy."

"It's a great family," Johnny said. "There's Ma now—in the doorway."

"I'll see you after supper then," Butch said.

"So you're gonna be a ballplayer," Smiley said after supper. "Ma tells me you're a painter, too. Paint a pretty good Indian, huh?" He broke into laughter.

Johnny grinned. "Yeah, I—well, it was kinda funny, huh?"

"Nancy's been painting too," Smiley said. "All afternoon. On a secret for you. She told Ma it's under your pillow."

And that was right where he found it, hours later when he finally crawled into bed for the night.

He was so tired and filled with ideas that he almost forgot. His arm ached from throwing and his back ached from stooping. And he had a whole boxful of jerseys to paint and another boxful of stencil paper and paints. And a whole handful of friends.

He was grinning to himself when he crawled into bed and saw the piece of paper sticking out from under his pillow. He pulled it out and sat on the edge of his bed unfolding it. It was a big heart with flowers all around it. And right in the middle it read, *I Luve You—Nancy.*

He refolded it carefully and put it in a drawer with his things. Then he lay down and stared at the ceiling. Way up through the ceiling to where God was. He knew He must be up there. *Thanks for everything,* he said. When he fell asleep, there was a smile on his face.

11

Where Were You Tuesday Night, Johnny?

"ALL RIGHT, JOHNNY," Smiley said, squatting down behind the plate. "It's a tie ball game, eighth inning. One out, and a man batting about .091 is at the plate. There's a runner on third and you're playing third. What do you look for?"

"That's too easy," Johnny said, slapping the ball into his mitt. "A suicide squeeze, of course."

"And where do you play?"

"Up close, to cover the bunt," Johnny said. He sailed the ball in to Smiley.

"Or tight on the bag, to get the man in a possible rundown. Which is it?"

"Up close, usually. Depends on the runner."

"And you expect a quick throw from the catcher when?"

"Anytime," Johnny said. "I've got to be ready

114

to take a throw at any time."

"Right. You're learning. And now I've got to go. I'll have to get back to the office by one today." He stood up, half turned, then whirled and whipped the ball down the third base line.

Johnny was taken completely by surprise and didn't even get a glove on it. He ran it down and came trotting back with it. By that time Smiley was standing by the gate grinning. "You said anytime, champ!"

Johnny broke into laughter. "Yeah, you got me that time. But honest, how'm I doin'?"

"Good. Real good," Smiley said. "You'll do all right in the game Saturday. Don't worry about it. Ricky'll be here for it, too, you know. He's making a trip down from camp."

"Boy, the guys really think a lot of him. Goggles is always talkin' about him, and Butch an— he's quite a guy."

"Yup," Smiley said. "And so are you, Johnny. It isn't always just the other guy who's a good guy, you know. And, unless I miss my bet, you're gonna be a mighty busy one too." He looked out at the front lawn.

"Yeah, I'm gonna mow it as soon as you go," Johnny said. He held up his hands. "Look at my blisters."

"Ma said you made nine dollars mowin' lawns yesterday. That's the old hustle."

"I'm gonna get a set of watercolors for Nancy," Johnny said. "She just loves to paint now; so I wanta get her her own set. I'm going down to the hardware this afternoon. I gotta go to the library."

115

"Library?"

"I need some books with lettering in them for the jerseys. The Indian heads look fine, but I need a pattern for the numbers and name."

"I saw them drying on the line last night," Smiley said. "You did a great job."

"It's a great team," Johnny said. "A great bunch of guys." He grinned. "I'm just happy I guess. I like it here."

"That's good," Smiley said. "But I really gotta get back to the office now, and you better get crackin' on that lawn." He jingled the coins in his pocket. "Before I go, I better give you your allowance."

"But, that's not till—"

"Well, maybe you'll wanta get yourself some paints too," Smiley said, digging out two dollars and giving them to him. "But I want the lawn edged too—a little trench cut around the sidewalks."

"Wait'll you see it," Johnny said. Just then the sun broke through and flooded the yard with sunshine. "Oh, no, a scorcher now, I'll bet."

And it was. When he had finally finished the lawn, it was nearly three o'clock, and his T-shirt was dripping with sweat. But he had done a good job. A real good job.

He left for the library whistling. *Yup, things had really turned out super!* It didn't seem possible that just a little over a month ago, he had been slaving away on the farm in Hastings...and then was mixed up in a bad jam with that Pete character...and jail...and Cleveland...and here he was, sitting on top of the world.

He felt so good he let out a *whoop!* and scared

an old woman who was watering her garden into dropping a bucket of water. He broke into laughter and dashed across the street, taking the shortcut to the library.

He rounded the corner and was just walking past the pay phone by the stoplight when someone called, "Johnny." *He knew that voice! It was—*

"Hello, son."

He whirled around and saw his dad stepping out of the phone booth. "I was just gonna call up there at the Knowles' and see if you wanted to come and see me."

"Hi, Dad," Johnny said, staring at him. He needed a shave and his clothes were rumpled and dirty. And he had been drinking again. "How—how did you know where—where to—"

"I talked to that Miss Crenshaw, and she said you were under the court now, so it'd be all right if she gave me your address."

"How do you feel?"

"Oh, I feel pretty good," Dad said. "My back's been hurtin' me a little." He grinned a little, and Johnny saw that he was pretty drunk, and probably had been for a couple days. "But I take a little medicine and—" He shrugged and stared at his feet. He had old, patched shoes on. "You still got your chain?" He fished inside his greasy shirt and pulled out the chain with the half-coin on it. "I got my half."

"And I got mine," Johnny said. "I never take it off."

"It got broke," Dad said, noticing the place where the ends had been tied together.

"Oh, I got in a fight and—"

"Did you whip him?" Dad said.

Johnny shrugged. "Not exactly, but I fought him. And he was a lot bigger than me. And—"

"That's my Johnny," Dad said. "Do you hear from your mother much?"

"Not—not since I was in that place," Johnny said. He frowned, thinking about the scene his mother had made. "But I oughta get a letter soon."

"Your mother and I both love you," Dad said. "And you've never heard me say a bad word against her, have you? And you never will. I loved your mother, but when you're older, you'll know that sometimes just loving someone isn't enough. And I—" He broke off suddenly and bent over, coughing heavily.

Johnny stared on helplessly. A moment later Dad stood up and wiped the tears from his eyes. "I—uh—uh—haven't been too well since I got out of that hospital. My back's been hurting." He glanced around. "You know those guys over there?"

Johnny looked over and saw Butch and Sam coming out of the drugstore, staring at them. "Yeah, I play ball with them."

"Well, I better get going. I wanta get some medicine and—" He stood there for a moment.

Impulsively Johnny dug in his pocket and fished out a five-dollar bill from his lawn-mowing money. *He'd still have enough for paints.* "Here, take this, Dad."

Dad looked at it, put his hand out, then stepped back. "No, no, I don't want your money, son. I don't—"

"A loan then," Johnny said. "For—for your—your medicine." He grinned. "Go ahead. I made twice that mowing lawns this week. You can pay me back when—when you feel well again and go back to work."

Dad took the bill. "Thanks, son. And I'll pay you back. Real soon. I'll send it by mail. I'd better go now. Your friends are coming over." Before Johnny could say anything more, he turned and walked off, limping a little.

"Who was that bum?" Butch said.

"Did you give him some money?" Sam did a quick shuffle. "See him limp? All them bums put on an act to—" He saw the look on Johnny's face and stopped suddenly. "Hey, what's the—"

"Shut up about that," Johnny said. "Just forget it!"

"Hey, what the—"

"Forget it!" Johnny said. "Don't try to make anything of it either!"

"Hey, I'm sorry," Sam said. "I was just kidding, okay?" He stuck out a hand. "Pals?"

Johnny nodded. "Yeah, I'm sorry. I just don't—don't like to see people make fun of—of sick folks. Come on now, I'm buyin'. Who wants a malt?"

They were just finishing their round of malts when Toughie Morrison came in. "Hey, I got good news!" he said, sliding in beside Sam. "We got a third baseman!"

"Where? Who did you get?"

"A new kid," Toughie said. "He just moved in with his aunt and uncle next door to me. I was playin' catch with him last night and boy, is he ever good! I mean—" he glanced over at Johnny. "If you?"

"Don't sweat about me," Johnny said. "I'm strictly a utility player and I know it. If you get a guy who can *really* play third base, that's fine with me. I'll just play utility. That's a hundred percent OK with me."

"We ain't pushin' you out," Butch said.

"If you really—"

"No, honest!" Johnny said. "If this guy is good, then I wouldn't have it any other way."

"He's up front getting a magazine," Toughie said. "Hey, Spider, come here."

Johnny's heart froze in his throat. *Could it be?*

It was.

Spider came walking over, the same slouching shuffle, the same cocky grin. Johnny let himself be introduced. *Don't say anything,* his eyes said, *and I won't either.* He caught just a trace of a nod that told him Spider had read his thoughts perfectly.

But the next half hour, sitting in the booth, his mind was in a turmoil. *What if they find out where I've been? What will they say? What if he tells them? Here everything had been going so great and now—now—now what?*

Finally he stood up. "I gotta get goin'," he said. "I have to get to the library yet." He glanced at Spider, hoping he would catch the hint. He did.

"I wanta get a card too," Spider said. "I'll walk over with you."

"Me and Butch will pick you up after supper then," Sam said. "We'll play a little ball tonight, okay? You too, Spider."

He waited until they were half a block down the street before he said anything to Spider. "Look, Spider, these guys don't know anything about my past, where I've been, and—"

"I'm not gonna tell on you," Spider said. "You can count on me. We can be pals now. I've got some ideas, too."

"What kind of ideas?" Johnny said.

"You'll see. It'll take time. I only got out three days ago."

They came to Drexler's Hardware. "I gotta get something here," Johnny said. "A set of paints."

"I wanted to buy something anyway," Spider said. "I need a good glove."

When Johnny went up to the counter to pay for his paints, the clerk was wrapping up a glove for Spider. "And here's your change," he said. "Sixty, seventy, seventy-five, a dollar, two, three, and four from fifteen. Anything else?"

"That's all," Spider said, stuffing the change in his pocket.

"How much did that glove cost?" Johnny said, as they walked out of the store. "Almost eleven bucks?"

Spider nodded. "A good glove is worth it." He fished it out, threw the bag away, and put it on. "I'm gonna oil it up as soon as I get home."

"But—"

"I get you," Spider grunted. "Well, my aunt has got lots of money and she gives me whatever I ask for. See? You believe me?"

"Yeah, sure," Johnny said. "I didn't mean—"

"Look, I'm not gonna tell on you, and don't you tell on me either. I mean, I was there too, you know. Okay?"

"Shake."

But still when Spider went left and he went right a block later, Johnny was worried. He didn't know why, but he had a feeling that something bad was going to happen. And then when he came down the street for home, and saw the plain black Chevy parked outside the house, he knew something really was wrong. It had a tiny aerial on the back, just like policemen used.

Or probation officers. Because when he walked in the front door, there was Red Fitzpatrick, arguing baseball versus football with Smiley. They both looked up when Johnny came in.

"Hi!" Johnny said, grinning. *He hadn't done anything, had he?*

"How you doin'?" Red said. "I hear you're gonna be a third baseman."

Johnny shrugged. "I try." He set the paints and the library books on the coffee table and squatted cross-legged on the davenport. "But there's this new kid and—" *Should he tell them about Spider? No.* "And we'll take turns," he finished.

"Everything going all right?" Red asked. "I see you did some shopping. What'd you get?"

"Some paints. For little Nancy—"

"He's gonna make an artist of her," Smiley broke in.

"Uh huh," Fitzpatrick said. "Tell me, where'd you get the money?"

"My allowance," Johnny said. "And I made nine bucks mowing lawns too. Didn't I, Smiley?"

"You sure did, son." Smiley turned to Fitzpatrick. "What's this about? You haven't told me anything either, you know."

Fitzpatrick rubbed a hand over his crinkly red hair. "Well, I'll make it brief. Where were you Tuesday night, Johnny?"

"Huh? I was down at the park playing ball."

"What time did you come home?"

He shrugged. "Dark, I guess. Around nine, wasn't it, Smiley? Remember, that was the night you and I were talking about painting the garage?"

"Yeah, he came home around nine o'clock," Smiley said. "A couple of his friends came with him. Why?"

"Well, a grocery store on the other side of the park was broken into and robbed that night and the police asked me to talk to Johnny about it."

"Me? Why me?"

Red looked at him. "You know, don't you?"

"Because I was in that place. Just because—but that isn't fair!"

"No, maybe it isn't," Red said. "But if you were home by nine, then you're okay. You didn't do it, did you?"

"No!"

"And if he says he didn't, then he didn't," Smiley said. "Johnny won't lie to you."

"That's good enough for me," Red said. "I just had to come and check it out—part of my job." He stood up. "I have to go now. This is an around-the-clock job and my wife almost forgets what I look like." He grinned. "I'll see you at the office next Tuesday, right?"

"Right."

After he was gone, Johnny sat poking through the paints he had bought for Nancy. Smiley came over and put a hand on his shoulder. "Don't let this bother you," he said. "We have faith in you, Johnny. This is your home."

Johnny looked up at him. "And I'm really happy here—happier than I've ever been." He thought of telling him about meeting his dad today, but found he was afraid to. *I'll just have to get used to that,* he thought. *Life just isn't made up of all good times.*

"Well, bedtime," Smiley said. "You say your prayers every night?"

"Sort of," Johnny said. "I mean, I think 'em."

"God hears that," Smiley said. "And—before you go—do you want to start Sunday school? We've got a real sharp bunch of guys there. Most of 'em you already know. But it's up to you. We won't push anything on you in this house, Johnny."

"Yep!" Johnny said. "I'll be there."

"Good," Smiley said.

And Johnny was smiling again when he went to bed. But then he started thinking about Spider and his dad and he wasn't smiling anymore. *I know it can't be all good times,* he thought. *But make it work out the way you want it to, God. And I'll try too. I'll try....*

12

Shut Up or I'll Tell on You!

FRIDAY was going to be a busy day. Johnny didn't wait to finish breakfast, but retreated to the basement with a plate of rolls and a half pitcher of milk. There was a ball game tomorrow, practice this afternoon—and that left him just the morning in which to finish stenciling fourteen baseball jerseys.

He had just laid out the first one on the work table, and was working his brush into the paint, when Tom-Tom came bouncing down the stairs. "Johnny! Come play ball with Tom-Tom."

"Can't!" Johnny said. "I'm busy."

"Pull-eeze!" Tom-Tom said, pulling at his arm. "Play catch with Tom-Tom."

"I can't! I've got to get this work done."

"You meanie!" Tom-Tom kicked him in the ankle hard.

"Yeoww! You little—" Johnny yelped, whirling around and grabbing him up by the collar. He started to slap him, but then caught himself. Tom-Tom was half crouched, eyes closed. Slowly, Johnny let him go and put a hand on his shoulder.

Tom-Tom looked up at him with wide brown eyes. "I'm sorry, Johnny. I didn't mean to kick you. I like you, Johnny."

Johnny ruffled his hair. "I like you too, Tom-Tom," Johnny said.

Tom-Tom was suddenly very grave and serious. "Do you? Honest? You *really* love Tom-Tom?" He made it sound like the most important thing in all the world.

Johnny nodded his head slowly. "You bet your britches I do, Tom-Tom."

"I like you, Johnny," Tom-Tom said. He turned toward the stairs. "I like you more'n anybody in the whole world, 'cept Ma and Smiley." He turned and raced suddenly up the stairs, leaving Johnny alone with his thoughts.

They were happy thoughts. Life was turning out to be pretty good after all, it seemed. He had a home now and a little brother and a little sister and Ma and Smiley and Rick—he'd be home from camp by suppertime, for the game tomorrow. But then there was Spider. He forced that thought out of his mind and concentrated on the jerseys. He'd have to work *that* out as it came along, playing it by ear.

He had the last shirt drying on the basement line when Butch poked his head in the stairwell and bellowed. "Calling all cars! Calling all cars! Come in, Nolan!"

"Is it noon already?" Johnny shouted back putting his paints away. "I'll be up and get my glove in a minute."

On his way upstairs, he picked up half a dozen jerseys that were fully dry and slung them over his shoulder. "I got six done," he said, "and the rest are drying out. They'll all be ready for the game tomorrow."

Butch plucked one off his shoulder and held it up for inspection. "Hey, keen! Goggles, come an' look at this." Goggles wandered in from the kitchen just then, munching a chocolate chip cookie he'd bummed from Ma. He stopped, cocked his head, and studied the jersey for a moment, then nodded his head in vigorous approval.

"Nice, huh?" Butch said. "Let's put ours on now."

"Yeah, they look sharp," Goggles said. "You did a swell job on them, Johnny."

"You might as well all have some cookies, at least, before you run off to play ball," Ma said, poking her head in the hallway. "I got soup on the stove."

"What time is it?" Johnny asked, pulling on a jersey.

"Time to eat!" Butch said.

Three dozen cookies and a pot of soup later they were on their way to Longfellow Park, playing catch back and forth in the street as they walked. Butch let a ball roll away and used the opportunity to walk back with Johnny. "Say, er—I was wonderin'," he said, looking down at his feet, "about this new kid—Spider. I mean, him playin' third and—"

"I told you it was all right," Johnny said. "Honest—if he can do a better job there, then let him play. I'll be happy just to play utility or anything."

"We just wanted to make sure—I mean, if you *want* to play—"

"It's okay." Johnny said, forcing a grin. "See if you can catch now. Run out for a grounder." He dropped back and let Butch get a lead on him. Goggles stood waiting at the corner a half block away. Then Johnny cut the ball loose, throwing as hard as he could. It sailed past Butch and cleared Goggles glove on the bounce. He walked on, thinking, while they chased it.

He found that, actually, he *did* mind a little. He knew he wasn't much good, but he'd never known what fun it was to play. And it seemed kinda mean or something for Spider to be the one to push him out of the way. Still, Spider was a lot better and—

It made him feel good, though, just to think of the way Butch and the guys had been so worried about hurting his feelings. That showed what a swell bunch of guys they were. Johnny couldn't imagine many of the guys he'd met in Cleveland being worried about how *he* felt. He managed to break into a grin by the time he caught up to Goggles and was just starting to tell him a joke Smiley had told him the night before when Butch came running up and pointed down the street.

"Hey, looka that!" Butch shouted. "Do you see what I see?"

They both stared and saw a kid pushing a wheelbarrow up the sidewalk toward them.

"It looks like—"

"Spider!" Johnny finished. "Why the wheelbarrow?"

"He's got something in it," Butch said. "Looks like—bats?"

Johnny squinted his eyes in the bright sunlight. "Bats? Yeah, it does look like bats sticking out. But—"

A minute later Spider came puffing up, pushing a small green wheelbarrow. And it was full of bats. And balls.

"Hey, you guys," Spider said with a grin. "Look what my aunt bought for the team!" He set the wheelbarrow down and stood their proudly, wiping the sweat off his brow.

"I told my aunt I was gonna be the third baseman for the Indians, and so she bought me all
this stuff—" He waved his arm over the wheelbarrow, a wide grin covering his face. "A dozen Louis-
ville Sluggers and a dozen brand-new baseballs. Quite
a haul, huh?"

"Yeah, that's keen!" Butch said, slapping him
on the back. "Boy, are we glad we got you on the
team. You must have a great aunt."

"This is just what we needed," Goggles said.
"Ain't this great, huh, Johnny?"

Johnny was a little surprised to find himself
feeling jealous. "Err—yeah. This is really great."

"Hey, I see you got your jerseys done," Spider
said, fingering the one Johnny had on. In the sunlight it was plain that it was a homemade job. "If
I'd known you needed them, I could have had my
aunt—"

"These are all right, ain't they?" Johnny said,
a little peeved. "I put a lot of work—"

"Yeah, whats wrong with them?" Goggles said.
"I like mine just the way it is."

Spider shrugged. "Well, if you ever need new
ones, just tell me and—"

Johnny changed the subject. Something sounded
wrong to him. *Or was he just jealous of Spider playing the big shot?* "Hey, there's Teddy and Denny
and some of the gang going into the park now," he
said, pointing down the hill a block ahead. "We
oughta get started. It must be one-thirty by now."

By the time the gang got over the surprise of
Spider showing up with a wheelbarrow of bats and
balls it was nearly two. And since it was just prac-

131

tice, Johnny got to play. Sort of, anyway. He got to lob in balls for Goggles to belt out for fielding practice.

As he pitched, he found his mind wandering back to Spider. Something seemed funny about him showing up with all those balls and bats. Johnny knew what they cost. But maybe he *did* have an aunt with lots of money. *Forget it. It's not your problem if he wants to be a big shot.* Or was he just jealous?

"Hey, wake up!" Goggles yelled. "That one went over my head!"

"Huh?" Johnny realized that he'd gotten so wrapped up thinking that he'd forgotten what he was doing. "Sorry. Toughie oughta be here pretty soon and take over anyway, huh? Ain't this what he usually does?"

Goggles lined the ball down the first base line. "Yeah, I wonder where he is. He's usually the first one here."

"Hey, here comes his brother now," Sam yelled. "Let's see what the deal is."

Toughie's brother was just a tall version of Toughie, with the same red hair, freckles, and wiry build. "Toughie won't be here today," he said when the guys came running up. "Mumps. And the doc says two weeks in bed."

A groan ran through the gang at the news. "Well, there goes our manager," Sam said. "Now what?" He turned and looked at Johnny. "Say—"

"Yeah," Butch said. "Maybe Johnny—"

"Sure, Johnny can manage the team," Goggles said.

"Me? But—but I don't—" Johnny stared around at them. "I—"

"You can do it, pal," Butch said. "It ain't that hard."

"Yeah," Teddy said. "Ricky said he'd be here for most of the games anyway. He can help you."

"The rules say we gotta have a manager," Butch said.

"Well, I'll try," Johnny said. "I mean, *Ricky* and I will try."

"Good enough!" Goggles said. "Now lob me in some more balls, boss!"

Johnny trotted back to the mound with a big grin. Was he the same dope who had been jealous of Spider a few minutes ago? *What a stupe!*

An hour later the jangling of a popcorn wagon broke up practice for the afternoon. "Hey, who wants a coke or something?" Spider yelled. "I'm buyin' today. My treat!"

Nobody could say no to that. Spider ended up buying cokes, popcorn, and ice-cream bars for the whole gang. Johnny saw him fish a bill out of a bulge in his pocket and caught Spider's eye. Spider grinned and winked at him. "Eat your popcorn and enjoy it," he said. "My aunt gives me all the spending money I want."

"Boy, I wish *I* had your aunt," Butch said.

"Yeah, man," Goggles echoed. "It sure must be rough."

"Yeah, it sure must be rough," Johnny said to Spider a half hour later, as they walked home together. He looked at his face to see if he had caught the sarcasm in his voice. "Your aunt must really have lots of dough."

Spider stopped and stared at him. "What are you tryin' to say?"

"Nothin'," Johnny said. "But my PO was over the other night. And he was asking me about a grocery store somebody broke into over on the other side of Longfellow."

Spider's eyes narrowed. "Your probation officer? What'd you tell him? Did you say anything about me?"

"No," Johnny said. "I never mentioned a thing about you."

"You better not," Spider said.

"What are *you* trying to say?" Johnny said, getting a little irked by the way Spider was talking.

"You just shut up about me," Spider said. "Or I'll tell on you. You think you're big cheese now, managing the team and all, huh? Well, what do you think the guys would say if they knew you were a jailbird?"

"Well, you were there *too!*" Johnny said.

"Maybe—" Spider said. "But I got an aunt that gives me money to buy balls and bats, and lots to spend on the guys. You don't."

"You can't buy—"

"You just shut up about me," Spider said, half yelling. "Or I'll tell on you. Then see how many friends you got. I know," he added with a trace of bitterness in his voice.

"I ain't gonna say nothin'," Johnny said. "Just forget it, okay?"

Spider shrugged. "Okay. But don't *you* forget. I gotta cut out now." He turned and cut up the alley, leaving Johnny standing there staring after him. Something was definitely rotten in Birchdale. But why should he worry about it? It wasn't his problem. Or was it?

Ricky was out back playing catch with Smiley when Johnny got home. "Hello, champ!" Rick said, lobbing the ball over to him. "Wanta give Smiley a break? Middle age is gettin' to him."

Smiley grinned. "I have to help Ma get supper ready," he said. "Don't you listen to this old-age talk." He turned to Ricky. "I'll arm wrestle you for dessert tonight, OK?"

"Not me," Rick said. "I take it all back."

"Boy, am I glad you showed up," Johnny said, taking a position behind the plate. "Toughie Morrison came down with the mumps and I got voted to manage the team."

"No kidding?" Ricky said. "I thought you were gonna play third."

"Well, there's this one kid, Spider, and—" Johnny hesitated. Should he tell Ricky? Everything? If he couldn't trust Ricky, who could he trust? He told him the whole story. Everything.

Ricky just stood there, scratching his head. "Well, what do *you* think? It sounds like you've already got him convicted and in jail." He threw the ball up in the air and caught it in his mitt. "Jumping to conclusions?"

Johnny scuffed a toe in the dirt. "I guess—I guess maybe I resent him a little, and I'm afraid he'll tell the guys on me, and—"

"I wouldn't worry about that," Ricky said. "I

135

know these guys pretty well, and I don't think they'd make a fuss about it. What you better worry about is how you feel about Spider."

"I guess—I guess I kinda resent him, and that's why I don't want to believe him, huh?"

"I'd pray about it if I were you," Ricky said. "That's what I do when I get a problem too big for me to handle. Try it."

"I—I don't—"

"Just try, Johnny," Ricky said. "God makes it pretty easy, if we just take that first step."

Johnny grinned up at him. "I'll try then. And—and *we* got a problem too, you know."

"Such as how to manage a baseball team?" Ricky winked. "I'll be right there with you. I can go over the basics tonight and tomorrow after the youth group meets at church. Did Smiley tell you about this?"

Johnny nodded. "He mentioned they'd meet tomorrow. Something about planning picnics for the summer."

Ricky put a hand on his shoulder. "You going? A great bunch of guys, and—"

"Sure. I'd like to join. I guess most of the guys on the ball team are in—"

"Five minutes till we eat!" Ma shouted, poking her head out the window. "Better wash up."

Nancy caught Johnny just as he was wiping his hands. "Come on, Johnny," she said. "I wanta show you something."

"But we're gonna eat now," Johnny said.

"It'll just take a min—utte! Come on."

Johnny grinned, and let Nancy pull on his shirt,

leading him into the sun room off the dining room. "Just a minute," she said, squatting down and sliding a sheet of paper out from under the old divan there. "I had to hide this, 'cause it's a secret."

"For who?"

"For Ma," Nancy said. She held it up. "Do you like it?" It was a crude drawing of a big fat woman with dark hair. And right in the middle of her chest was a big red heart. Lettered across the top were the words: *Luve from Nancy*.

"It's very nice," Johnny said. "Ma will really like it."

"Don't tell," Nancy said. "It's a secret; so don't you tell."

Don't tell—don't tell—don't tell. The words rang in his mind as he walked in to dinner. What if Spider told? What if—*don't tell!*

13

It's the Hospital, Johnny, Your Dad

GOING to the youth group meeting at church Saturday morning turned out to be pretty much the same as going to Longfellow Park to play ball. The same gang of guys showed up. When Johnny walked up the elm-shaded walk to the yard next to the flagstone-faced church, he saw at least a dozen familiar faces among the twenty or so kids clustered about—boys in one big knot, and girls giggling in twos and threes.

"A great bunch of kids," Ricky said. "I'm going in and see Pastor Winthrop for a few minutes. Meeting won't start for a half hour anyway." He paused, then spoke in a lower voice, looking Johnny square in the eyes. "Did you do what I asked you to?"

Johnny nodded. "Yeah."

"And it helped, didn't it?"

"Yeah, it—it did," Johnny mumbled. "See ya later." He turned and hurried over to the big elm, where Goggles, Butch, and a few other guys were gabbing. *I didn't really pray*, he thought. *Not the way Ricky meant.* But he had tried. He had really tried. But he just couldn't stop his worrying. *What would these guys think if they knew? What if Spider told them?* He looked up to see Butch and Goggles waving at him and forced a grin. *But would they be waving at him if they knew all about him?*

"Hey, did you hear the news?" Goggles said excitedly.

"About Terry's dad," Sam said, pointing to Terry, standing a few feet away and talking excitedly with Butch and Teddy. "His store got robbed!"

"Robbed?"

Goggles nodded. "Yeah, someone broke into the place last night and— Here's Terry now. Terry, tell him about it."

"Yeah, someone broke into my dad's store last night," Terry said. "Dad went down there early this morning. He forgot some papers there yesterday. And when he got there—"

"He found the door busted in, huh?" Goggles broke in.

"*I'll* tell him, goofus," Terry said. "Yeah, someone broke the back door—we got a door with panels in it—and someone pried the panel loose and crawled in."

All Johnny could think was, *How long before Red Fitzpatrick comes to question me?* He knew he had to say something, though. "Uh—uh—what did he take?" *He almost said Spider.*

"Dad ain't sure yet," Terry said. "But it was more'n a hundred bucks, at least. The money in the cash register."

"Boy, that's three I know of right around here lately," Goggles said.

"Three?"

"Yeah, didn't you hear about the gas station over on Xerxes? Someone broke a window there Wednesday night and took about fifty bucks. And I guess the Cut-Cost Grocery, over by the park, got burgled last week."

"Wow! We got a burglar around here someplace," Goggles said. He turned and stuck a thumb in Sam's ribs. "Okay, Buster. You're under arrest. We know you did it!"

"No. Help! I'll never squeal, copper!" Sam yelped in a mock tough-guy manner. "You ain't got nothin' on me."

They both broke out laughing and Johnny managed to force a half smile, but he didn't feel like laughing. And he was glad a few minutes later when Ricky and the pastor came to the door to signal them to come in for the meeting. He took a seat in the back and tried to pay attention to what was going on. But twice the guy next to him, a kid he didn't know, had to elbow him when it was time for a vote for something. Johnny raised his hand both times, but he never knew what he was voting for— or against. All he could think was Spider, Spider, Spider!

It had to be Spider, didn't it? Or did it? Maybe it was just an odd coincidence, huh? But what would he tell Fitzpatrick? Should he tell him about Spider?

140

Maybe he really did have an aunt who gave him money, and maybe he didn't. But, should he tell? It wasn't his business, was it. Or was it? Johnny just didn't know and he was afraid to ask. Maybe he should have told Smiley before. Maybe it would do more harm than good now to tell. And, if he told on Spider, maybe it would all come out about him then and what would his new friends think? He just didn't know.

And when he and Ricky left for the ball game after dinner, he still didn't know. Smiley had had to beg off at the last minute, to finish painting the garage. They walked in silence for a block, then Ricky said: "What's buggin' you, pal?"

"Nothin'," Johnny said quickly.

Ricky stopped and looked directly at him. "You don't mean that and you know it. What is it?"

"Spider," Johnny said. "I'm afraid that—"

"That he'll tell these guys where you were? Is that all you're worried about?"

"Er—uh—" Johnny knew that was only half of it. But he decided to hear what Ricky had to say, before he said any more. "Well, yeah, I'm worried about that. Yeah."

"If you knew Butch and Goggles and these guys as well as I do, you wouldn't worry at all," Ricky said. "What do you say to this. I'll tell them about you, in a nice way, and then—"

"No!" Johnny said. "Don't say anything! Just forget it!"

"Take it easy, pal," Ricky said. "Just trust me a little, will you? I wouldn't even suggest this if I didn't *know* just how these guys—"

Johnny shook his head vigorously. "No, don't say a word! Just forget all about it!"

Ricky shrugged. "If that's what you want. But—" They walked the rest of the way to the park in silence.

Johnny wondered if maybe Ricky hadn't had the right idea. *But could he take the chance? He had a good bunch of pals now. Why even risk losing them?* He'd trusted people before and regretted it. He just didn't know what to think. *Why did life have to be such a tangled up mess?*

Most of the guys were already out on the diamond practicing when they got there. And the other team, the Roseville Dodgers, were on the diamond catercorner to theirs, warming up.

"What do I do now?" Johnny asked, suddenly realizing that he was going to start having to put into practice the theory Smiley and Ricky had been drilling into him the past week.

"Make up your score sheet and batting order," Ricky said, "and turn your batting order in to the umpire. Simple enough?" He grinned and handed him the notebook he had been carrying under his arm. "It's all yours now, pal. I'm strictly an adviser."

Johnny had no trouble making up a batting order. There was only one player for each position— except third base—but, as manager, he couldn't list himself as a player. That left him with just one extra player, Terry, who could pitch in a tight spot, in which case Sam would take over in left field for him.

Spider was there all right. The first thing Johnny saw was that he had on brand-new baseball shoes. Spider came walking over, grinning. "Like my new spikes?"

"My aunt—" Spider began.

Johnny frowned, pretending that he was much busier making out his batting order than he actually was. "They must have cost you a lot."

Johnny glared up at him. "Where was your aunt last night? Breaking into Terry's dad's clothing store, huh?"

Spider grabbed him by the shirt front. "What you tryin' to say?" His eyes narrowed. "You got a big mouth for such a little guy."

Johnny jumped up and pushed him away. "You didn't know about the place getting robbed, huh?"

Ricky started walking toward them. Spider dropped his arms. "Sure—Goggles and Sam told me. They never accused me of doing it. Why should you?"

"Well, those things you bought, and you were in—"

"So were you," Spider said. "And if you wanta tell stories, I can tell a story or two about you, you dig me?" He grinned. "Let's just be friends, huh, jailhouse buddy?"

"Forget it then," Johnny said. "I won't say a word to anyone. And don't you—"

"I'll be just as quiet as you," Spider said.

"Everything okay here?" Ricky asked.

Spider winked. "All burners cookin'," he said.

"Yeah, I've got my order set up," Johnny said.

"Then let's play ball," Ricky said. "The umpire wants your card." Spider walked off, then trotted out to third base. "You *sure* everything is all right?" Ricky asked, once he had gone.

"Let's play ball, huh?" Johnny said. "I said everything is just fine and dandy."

Ricky let it go at that and the ball game started. Sam got through the first inning easily, giving up only a little infield dribbler. When the team came to the bench for their turn at the plate, Spider was talking a mile a minute. "We win this game, I'll buy everybody malts and burgers after the game."

"Wow! I'm goin' three for four today, at least!" Butch said.

"Make it two hamburgers," Goggles said. "And I'll get five RBI's."

"My aunt gave me money—so, if we win, I'll buy it all." He looked over his shoulder and winked at Johnny. "We gonna win, pal?"

Johnny clenched his teeth and nodded. "Terry, they want you in the on-deck circle." He looked at Ricky. "Right?"

"Right." Ricky caught Johnny staring at Spider's back. "Just tend to the ball game now," he said.

Johnny caught the hint and grinned sheepishly.

Three innings slipped by. The promise of hamburgers and malts had an effect, because when the Indians took the field for the top of the fourth, they owned a solid 5-1 lead.

"How'm I doing?" Johnny asked.

"Fine. Just fine," Ricky said. "Just keep it up, and keep your mind on the game. That's all you got to worry about now."

Johnny grinned. "I get the message."

"Hey!" Ricky said. "Isn't that Tom-Tom?" He

pointed out across the field to a little boy, running toward them.

"Yeah, it is," Johnny said. "I wonder what—"

"Johnny! Johnny!" Tom-Tom yelled. "Smiley says come home. Right now."

"What—"

"The hospital," Tom-Tom said. "They call up. The hospital, Johnny; it's your dad!"

14

Get the Hurt Out, Johnny

DAD WAS DEAD. By the time they got to the hospital, Johnny knew it was too late. It was written all over Smiley's face. And he didn't feel anything. He was just numb all over. He sat waiting in the noisy emergency waiting room lobby, staring at the pattern on the tile floor, not noticing the noise and flurried activity that swirled around him. Even before Smiley came back from talking with the doctors in the hallway, Johnny just knew what he was going to say: *I'm sorry, Johnny, but your dad....*

When he finally came back, he put a hand gently on his shoulder, and spoke in a low voice. "Let's go home, son." Together they walked out to the car in silence. There was nothing that had to be said, just then.

Smiley drove a while in silence until they were

147

out of the heart of the city. Then he pulled off onto a side street—a quiet, tree-shaded place—and parked. He sat there, his hands holding the wheel tightly, waiting for Johnny to say something, to cry, to let go of the hurt.

"How—what—how did it happen?" Johnny said. His lips felt stiff, like the time he had gotten novocaine from the dentist. "Was—"

"He was hit by a car crossing the street," Smiley said in a low voice. "There wasn't a chance to save him. He—had been—drinking—"

"He's dead," Johnny said, snapping his fingers. "Just like that and he's dead. I never thought it could be—that—easy. Just like that and my dad is dead." He sat staring out the window straight ahead, wanting to cry, but somehow not being able to. He didn't want to look at Smiley, or talk to him, or do anything. He just wanted to sit quietly, staring at nothing, while he tried to make himself understand that suddenly he didn't have a father anymore.

"He didn't leave much," Smiley said, fumbling in his pocket. "Just this." He held out a crumpled up envelope and a metal chain with a half-coin dangling from it. "He had the chain in his hand when they found him."

Johnny nodded and unfolded the dirty envelope. On the outside, in spite of the dirt, he could read his name and the Knowles address. Inside the envelope was a wrinkled dollar bill and two fifty-cent pieces. He stared at them for a moment, then remembered the money he'd loaned Dad that day on the sidewalk. Carefully he folded the envelope, put it in his pocket, and sat there with the chain in his hand, rubbing the smoothness of the coin between his thumb and forefinger.

"This was—something. Like a—a sort of secret we had," he said. He fished inside his shirt and pulled out his own coin. He sat there, trying to fit the two halves together. But they didn't quite fit. No matter how much he turned them, this way and that, they didn't quite fit.

It seemed to mean something to him. Maybe that was how his mom and dad had been, like two halves of a coin that just didn't fit. Maybe that was what he was, someone who wouldn't ever fit. Maybe— He shook his head and jammed the coins, chain and all, into his pocket, and stared out the window. After a while he spoke, and he was surprised to find how small his voice sounded in the silence that seemed to surround him now. "Let's go home. Ma and Ricky will be wondering what—" He didn't say the rest.

Smiley hesitated, and Johnny knew that he was waiting for him to cry. But he didn't have any tears.

"Don't you—maybe you should pray now," Smiley said, finally. "It's not good to hold the hurt in like that."

"I can't," Johnny said coldly. "He wouldn't hear me." He sat there rigidly, clenching and unclenching his fists. "Just leave me be and I'll be all right."

Slowly Smiley started the car and drove off. Johnny rode home in a numb silence. And, for some reason, the only thing he could think of didn't really make sense at all. The thought that filled his mind was the fact that the two halves of the coin didn't quite fit together.

Somehow the next three days drifted past. Sunday came, and he went to church, but didn't hear the sermon. He didn't forget to pray, but he wasn't sure what he was praying for, or why. Life went on. He ate and slept. Ricky went back to camp on Monday. Nancy cut her thumb on a can opener. Tom-Tom got into another fight with the kids up the street. Ma baked six pies for the Ladies' Aid. Smiley went to work every day.

And his dad was still dead, and he couldn't cry.

Johnny walked around as though he were in a trance, numb and cold inside. He ate his food, but never knew what it was. He knew that Ma and Smiley were waiting for him to say something, to take the first step. But he was just numb and cold, and he didn't want to do anything but sit and wait for the pain to go away.

Wednesday came. He got up, dressed, and ate breakfast. Ma was quiet, and Nancy and Tom-Tom kept the silence they had held around him ever since the day he'd come home from the hospital. Then Ma sat down across the table from him. "Are you going to play ball today?" she asked. "I talked to Butch's mother last night, and she was wondering if Butch should come over yet. He wasn't sure if he should because—"

"I don't want to," Johnny said. "I don't want to do anything."

"Johnny, Johnny," she said, shaking her head from side to side. "Life has to go on. We have to go on living. You just can't stop living."

"But—but—why—why did this have to happen? Why—"

"I don't know," Ma said. "I couldn't begin to tell you. But I know you can't keep it bottled up inside yourself. If you can't tell me, then tell God. He'll listen."

"I tried to. I really did," Johnny said. "But—I—I just couldn't. I just couldn't."

After that Ma didn't have anything more to say. And when Butch came over, Johnny stayed home and let the guys play ball without him. After lunch he went out in the yard and took his paints along. Maybe he could paint.

He set everything up slowly and carefully. But he found that he couldn't paint either. He just sat there staring at the canvas.

"Johnny, can I watch you?"

"Huh?" He looked up to see Nancy watching him, standing shyly a few feet away. "No, I'm not going to paint," he said. He realized his voice was harsher than he meant it to be. "I'm sorry, honey, but I—"

She came walking over and patted his shoulder. "Don't cry, Johnny," she said. "Mom told me your daddy's resting now—just like he went to sleep. There's nothing we can do to bring him back."

Johnny sat there, staring right through her. He couldn't think of anything to say. He looked and saw that she was on the verge of tears herself.

"Hey, hey, Button-nose," he said. "Don't *you* cry."

She sniffed. "I feel bad when I see you feel bad," she said. "Don't worry, Johnny. Just sitting around pitying yourself won't help." She turned and walked off, leaving him feeling more confused and alone than ever. *Why couldn't he believe the way she did?*

She was only a little kid, he told himself. But the thought kept nagging him that she was right and he was wrong. He got up and walked around the yard, kicking at the dirt. Then he sat down and attacked his paints furiously, as though he could paint the hurt away.

He was still trying to paint an hour later when he heard the slam of a car door out front and looked up to see a cab pulling away. A moment later Ricky came walking around the back of the house, a duffel bag in his hand. "Hi, pal! I thought I'd take a day off and see how you were feeling."

Johnny nodded, and got up to walk over to him. "Just like that, and you took a day off?"

"I thought—" Ricky stared at his feet. "Well, Ma called me at camp last night. She told me you— you know."

"Just leave me alone and I'll be all right," Johnny said.

"Will you?" Ricky challenged. "Maybe you want this to last as long as you can make it last. Maybe you like feeling like a martyr, huh? Maybe—"

"Is that what you came for?" Johnny snapped, feeling his temper starting to mount. "To pick on me?"

Ricky grabbed him by the shoulder and stared into his face. "Look, Johnny, your dad is dead. He was drunk, and he got hit by a car, and now he is dead, and you'll never see him again. Do you really understand that?"

"Leave me alone! He was the best dad in the world! Leave me alone!" He pushed away, but Ricky held him fast.

"No, I won't leave you alone, Johnny. Not now. That part of your life is over, and you've got to weep for it, and then put it away. Your dad is dead, and you've got to let the past go."

"Leave me alone! Don't talk about it! Let go!" Johnny tried to break free and run, but Ricky was too strong. He held him by the shoulders, face to face.

"Leggo! Lemmeego!" Johnny kicked him in the shins as hard as he could, lowered his head on his chest, and rained blows on his face. "I hate you! I hate you! I hate everybody! My dad's dead! He was the only one in the whole world who loved me and he's dead." He swung furiously, kicking and screaming and sobbing all at once, while tears coursed down his face.

Ricky stood there, soaking up the punishment. In a moment the dam broke and Johnny fell forward, leaning on Ricky while great sobs racked his chest. "He's dead, Ricky. He's dead! My dad's the only one who loved me, and he's dead!"

Ricky held an arm around him, and ran his other hand through his hair. "Get the hurt out, Johnny. Sometimes it's hard, but you've got to get the hurt out so you can go on living. Your dad loved you, and that was good, whatever else he was or did. And it's right that you should cry for him." He stood there holding Johnny, staring at nothing. "But—but life has to go on. You've got to get the hurt out and then go on living."

The sobs gave way to sniffling, and then Johnny was able to sit down and talk with Ricky. "I didn't want to hurt you," he said. "I—I don't—don't know. I didn't mean what I said—I—"

"I know it," Ricky said. "I made you do it. I—I had to get the hurt out once too. You wanted to beat up the whole world, but you couldn't. So I let you use me instead." He grinned a little. "You've got a pretty fair left hand too."

Johnny grinned back and realized that it was the first time he'd been able to smile since it had happened.

"He might not have been much," Johnny said soberly. "But—but he was all I had." He broke off the thought and stood up. "That's over, I guess. You're right, Ricky. Life has to go on." He paused, then broke into a half grin. "And we've got another ball game this week. As long as you're home, you might as well get your glove out."

But it hurt; it still hurt. And Johnny knew that it would be a long, long time before the hurt was gone. Till then, he could live with it.

And something else hurt too—Mom. She had never called, never come to see him, never written. In the back of his mind, ever since it had happened, Johnny had felt that he was going to hear from her. But he hadn't and, somehow, that hurt too.

The next day he found out why. He was just leaving the house after supper to meet Butch and Sam at the park when Ma called him back. "I forgot all about this," she said, handing him a big, fold-out postcard. "The mailman brought it this morning, and I clean forgot it."

He walked down the street, staring at the picture. It looked like a big resort hotel on the ocean. He opened it up and caught the signature: *Mom.*

Slowly, he read it:

Surprise! George and I are on our honeymoon, honey. We've been married since Saturday. Sorry I didn't tell you, but we weren't sure until the last moment. Will write soon. In the meantime, be good and try to stay out of trouble. I'm sorry for bawling you out that time, but you don't know how it hurt me to see you in jail. I don't ever want to see you in jail again.

Love,

Mom.

He stood there, staring at it, stunned. He wasn't surprised by her getting married. He'd known she and George had been planning that. But to think that she had had to worry in a postcard about him being in that place! And *she* was hurt to see him there.

Angrily, he crumpled the card up in his hand and was about to throw it away when he saw Butch, Sam, and Spider coming up the street. He jammed it into his shirt pocket and tried to put it out of his mind. But the thought stayed with him—*she* was hurt!

"Hey, kid, how's everything," Butch said, grinning. "Feel ready to get back in the groove?"

"Sure do," Johnny said.

"Hear what happened since—since then," Sam said, a little embarrassment showing in his face. "I mean, well—"

"Don't worry about—that," Johnny said. "Just tell me the big news."

"Burglars again!" Butch interrupted.

"Yeah! They broke into two more places Tuesday night—a gas station and the hardware store on Lennox Avenue."

Johnny stared around, not knowing what he was expected to say. Spider was standing back a little, half grinning at him, as though they had a secret to share.

"No kiddin'?" Johnny said. "Funny the cops ain't got him yet."

"I hear they saw him once," Sam said. "They say it's just a kid. Someone saw him leaving the gas station."

"No kiddin'?" He searched Spider's face.

"Let's play ball," Spider said suddenly. "Come on, you guys. He threw the ball high in the air. "Catch!"

Johnny and Sam took the cue at the same time and collided under the ball. Johnny flew one way and Sam the other. By the time he sat up, he saw that the postcard had fallen out of his pocket. Even as he reached for it, Butch was picking it up. "Hey! Look at this hotel. Who do you know in Florida?"

Johnny leaped up and made a grab for it. "Gimme that!"

"Secrets?" Butch said teasingly, stepping back and opening the card. "Hey, jail?" He looked at Johnny quizzically. "What's this about jail?"

"None of your nosy business!" Johnny yelled, grabbing for the card.

"Jail?" Sam said. "Were you in jail, pal?"

"Maybe *you're* the burglar, huh?" Butch said. His voice made it plain that he was teasing, but Johnny didn't take it that way. "Johnny, the jail-bird burglar! Ha-ha—"

"No, I ain't! I ain't!" Johnny screamed, swinging wildly at him.

"Hey, I was just kiddin'!"

"Yeah," Spider said. "Don't blow up, burglar boy. Ha-ha!"

Johnny whirled around. "*You* got a lot of room to talk. You were in that place too. And—and—" His face twisted in fear and rage as he blurted out: "You're the burglar, Spider! Your aunt never gave you any money!"

Butch and Sam stood there, watching them in awkward silence. Spider spoke first. "I always knew you were a dirty snitch rat, Nolan. And now I'm gonna beat your ugly head in!" He advanced on Johnny, waving his fists menacingly. "You dirty snitch rat!"

Johnny stood there hesitantly, not knowing what to do. He could see his whole world crashing down around him just when it had seemed that the worst was over. *Nothing was going to turn out right after all. It was all going to end up in a mess, just like everything always did.*

He turned suddenly and began running up the hill, out of the park, and down the street, not knowing where he was going and not caring. Behind him he could hear the steady patter of Spider's feet chasing him and the shrill threats and curses.

A sudden blaring of a horn startled him, and he realized that he was running down the middle of the street. He looked up to see a coming car swerve to the curb, and he bounded to the sidewalk on the other side of the street. Out of the corner of one eye he saw the car was plain and black, and he caught what looked like an aerial on the back fender. He almost imagined that he saw a big, bluff redhead behind the wheel. But he didn't care, and he didn't look back.

The horn squalled for a moment, drowning out Spider's curses. But Johnny just shook his head and dodged down an alley. A moment later there was no sound but the patter of his footsteps and the echo of Spider's close behind him. Johnny just kept running.

15

Just One Chance, Please God!

SPIDER caught him four blocks away. And Johnny didn't even care. He was panting, and out of breath, and stumbled over the curb. A moment later Spider landed on his back. "Now I got you, you dirty cheese rat!" He threw an arm around Johnny's head and began pounding him on the back and neck.

Johnny rolled to one side, squirming and kicking, and managed to wiggle free. For a second he was tempted to run, but he was too tired. Instead, he lunged headfirst into Spider, grabbing him around the waist, and they went tumbling into the street.

A moment later they were both winded, and they broke it up and sat there, staring at one another in a wary silence. Johnny spoke first. "I—I—guess maybe I shouldn't have said anything. I goofed, I guess."

"Yeah, you really fixed things up good," Spider said. "What do you think they think of us now? Of you?" He spit between his feet. "I don't need them anyway."

"I—I don't—" Johnny couldn't think of anything to say. *Had the guys just been teasing him or had they been serious? Or worse?* He wasn't so sure now, not at all. "A plague on them then, if that's how they want to be." *No! He didn't mean that, and he knew it. But he had said it, hadn't he?*

"Let's forget it," Spider said. "No harm done yet. I hope."

"If you wanta," Johnny said. "Maybe you never did rob those places. I don't know why I said that. You didn't rob them, did you?"

Spider winked at him and grinned. "I don't know—did I?" He dug in his jeans and fished out a crumpled pack of cigarettes. "Let's go for a walk and have a smoke."

"I didn't know you smoked," Johnny said. His voice sounded odd to him, and his mind dredged up a memory of Pete—and— He forced the thoughts back.

"Not around these goody-goody sissies I don't," Spider said, leading the way into the alley. He lit a match and the glow set off his face like a mask in the early darkness. "They don't know what the score is. They ain't been around like we have, huh, jailhouse buddy?"

"Don't call me that!" Johnny half shouted. "I— I don't like that."

"Why not? Here, have a weed."

Johnny pretended not to hear him and looked

160

at his feet as they walked slowly down the alley. "I—Oh, hang it! Maybe you're the only friend I've got now, for all I know." *A voice seemed to say... Ricky...Goggles....Sam...*

"You bet I am," Spider said, pushing the cigarette at him again. "And don't you forget it. I called you a snitch, but I don't think you are, not really. You wouldn't cheese on me, would you?"

Johnny took the cigarette and looked at it. "I don't know anything to snitch about," he said finally in a low voice. He held the cigarette at arm's length, staring at it.

Spider grinned. "Good thinkin'. Now, you gonna smoke that butt or play with it? You ain't chicken, are you? Afraid of what Butch and all the goody-goodies would say?"

Johnny stared at the cigarette. Somehow, it seemed very important whether he smoked it or threw it away. He kept thinking of Pete—and all the memories that went with that.

"Well?" Spider said, lighting a match and holding it in his cupped hands.

Johnny stuck the butt in his mouth and let Spider light it.

"It's almost dark out," Spider said. "I know how we can have some fun." He gave Johnny a sideways look. "And I don't mean breaking into some store."

Johnny looked at the cigarette in his hand, then at Spider.

"Yeah?"

Johnny shrugged. "Nothing." But he meant something. Only he didn't know how to say it—yet. He hoped he would, when the time came.

"Come on," Spider said. "Let's walk."

Coming out of the alley, they saw an old woman staring at them, and Johnny threw his cigarette behind him. Spider looked at him and grinned. "What's the matter?" He took a big drag and blew the smoke at the old woman, who stared at them for a moment, then turned into a house.

"Forget it," Johnny said.

Spider shrugged and they kept walking.

Twenty minutes later it was fully dark and they were on a side street in a neighborhood a mile or more from the park. Spider led the way, looking up and down side streets carefully, while Johnny trudged behind, his hands jammed in his pockets.

"Hey, there's a couple now," Spider said, stopping suddenly and pointing up a side street. "Let's get 'em."

Johnny stared. "Get what?"

"Come on," Spider said, running halfway up the street. He stopped and stared back at Johnny. "If you ain't scared," he sneered. "You know, I *could* go back and just tell Butch and Goggles and them *all* about you, and then they wouldn't have a doubt in the world about you. Right now they aren't sure."

Johnny felt numb. He didn't know what Spider had in mind, but he didn't seem to care. *It didn't matter now, did it?* Nothing seemed to. "I ain't scared." But his voice told him he was.

They got to the corner, crossed the street, and then he saw what Spider was talking about. A pair of parked cars, one in the ring of light cast by the street light, and one in the darkness just beyond.

Spider looked around carefully. "You know what

jockey-boxing is?"

"I got a hunch."

"It's real easy. People leave stuff in their cars, in the glove box, or on the seat, and we find it. Finders keepers, losers weepers." He tiptoed up to the car and tried the door. "It's locked. You go around the front and try the other side."

Johnny stood staring at him. "I—err—"

"Come on!" Spider growled. "Now."

"The light," Johnny said finally. *What was he doing here? He didn't want to do this. Things did matter!*

Spider grunted and scooped up some gravel from the street. "Fix that easy enough." His first peg was short, but the second was right on target. There was a sudden blackness, followed by the tinkle of falling glass. "Let's get going now," Spider said. "Before someone reports the light."

"I see something," Johnny said, staring between two houses across the street. *Did he really see something? Or did he want to see something?*

"Quit stallin'," Spider hissed. "You ain't gonna chicken out now, are you?"

"I—" Johnny stopped and stared. "I—yes—I AM CHICKEN! I'm not going to do it." Things did matter; people did care! It wasn't too late. What had Ricky said? *When you need help, God's always there.* He clenched his teeth, staring at a point just in front of his feet, forming the words in his mind: *Dear God ... just give me this one chance to make things right ... just on chance ... please!*

Spider's face was cold and hard in the weak light. "Why, you yellow, phony, rotten punk! So you

163

chickened out! You dirty snitch rat!" He put his hands on his hips and stared at Johnny. "I'm not askin' again. Are you with me or not?"

Johnny stared back at him, not at his feet any longer. His mind was filled with a rush of memories: *Pete . . . the jail in Hastings . . . Ma . . . Smiley . . . Ricky . . . Tom-Tom . . . Nancy . . . all his friends. All his friends! And his home! His home!*

"Don't do it, Spider. Let's go back. It's not too late! We can—"

"Dirty cheese rat snitch. Nolan, you stink!" Spider spit at him, then pushed him suddenly, and Johnny fell backward over the curbing. "If you snitch on me, I'll bend a baseball bat on your head." Spider started to pull open the car door.

"Don't do it," Johnny said, scrambling to his feet. "It's not too late. You've still got a chance, Spider. I can get Smiley to help you. I—don't do it. Things *do* matter. They do!"

Spider turned and sneered at him. "Who cares?"

"God cares!" Johnny said. He had prayed for the right words and found them. "I care. And—"

"Get away!" Spider said, getting into the car.

"But—no—don't do it." Johnny grabbed Spider around the back, and started to pull him out of the car. "It's not too late," he panted, dragging him back. "Don't give up now. I'll help—"

Spider whirled and rammed an elbow into his stomach. "No! You—you're just like all the rest. You—you!" Spider let out a choked scream and lunged at Johnny, shouting and kicking and crying all at once. "I hate you, Nolan! I hate you all— all of you!"

Johnny was caught off balance and they went
tumbling into the street, bathed in the light from a
car. Johnny heard the clatter of feet, and then the
squeal of tires. The first thing he saw was Spider's
face, close to his. He was no longer fighting. He was
hunched up, choking and crying.

"I seen 'em," a voice called out. "I seen everything, officer!"

Johnny looked up to see a heavyset man in a
T-shirt, standing next to a policeman, pointing at
them and chattering. A second policeman came
over and dragged him to his feet. "Let's go, boys."

An hour later Johnny was sitting on the edge
of the bunk, in a dreary, gray precinct station cell.

He hadn't seen Spider since they'd come down to the station—he and Spider in the back of the squad car, the two policemen and the other man in front. A detective had come to get Spider as soon as they'd gotten to the jail.

Johnny sat there, trying to think. *I'm right back where I started at.* No, he wasn't. Somehow, he knew, things were different. He thought of the last time he had been in jail. And how he'd prayed. And this time he'd prayed first and still come to jail. And what had come of it?

Suddenly it struck him what *had* come of it. Why, he *had* gotten everything he wanted! He jumped up and began walking around the cell. He still *had* everything he wanted—Ma...Smiley... everything!

Or did he?

God had given him all the good things and the bad ones were his own choosing. *But I tried.* At the back of his mind, a voice seemed to say, *"Did you? How hard?"*

But always he had held something back. And this time he knew that he hadn't. Johnny knew that now, no matter what else happened, he was ready to take that big step, and just trust God for all the little steps after that. He just sat down quietly on the edge of the bed and whispered, "I'll trust you, God. You just lead me, and I'll do anything you show me to do. Just make this all come out right and—and—and if it doesn't, then I'll know that you have another plan for me."

He lay back and, somehow, felt restful and almost happy.

When he woke up the next morning, Johnny felt strangely peaceful. But then he had a visitor. Fitzpatrick. As soon as he walked in, Johnny knew that he was the one he had seen when he had run out of the park. Before he could say anything, Fitzpatrick sat down and half grinned at him. "Well?"

Johnny shrugged.

"I've got news," Fitzpatrick said. "Some of it's bad. Spider confessed to all the burglaries down by the park, and—"

Johnny stared at him. Something seemed wrong here.

"And he named you, Johnny. He said that you were with him on all the burglaries!"

16

Let's Go Home Now, Johnny

JOHNNY stared at Fitzpatrick. "No! He's lying! I never was! It's all a lie! I—"

Fitzpatrick nodded his head rapidly. "I told you once I'd trust you to tell me the truth, Johnny. And I will now. I think you ought to know—"

Johnny didn't even hear him. All he could think was, *Nothing will come out right after all!* "No! Spider just wants to get me in trouble. He wants to get even with me because—"

"You never robbed anyplace with him?"

"Last night was the only time I was with him. And *he* wanted to do it. I wouldn't help him. I tried—"

"Whoa! Just take it easy," Red said, breaking out into a half grin. "Just back up again and tell me about last night. I saw you running out of the

168

park with Spider after you yesterday when Ricky and I came driving up—"

"Then it *was* you I saw!"

Red nodded. "We'll talk about that later. But, what about this car that Spider was breaking into last night? You and Spider, maybe I should say?" He cocked his head to one side and looked at Johnny hard. "Or shouldn't I?"

"No! I wouldn't help. I told him to stop. I—"

Fitzpatrick held up a hand. "I wanted to hear you say it. Do you know a man named Shapiro?"

"Mr. Shapiro? No." Johnny shook his head. "I—"

"Come on." Fitzpatrick opened the door and led the way from the cell, down the hall to a visiting room at the far end. When Johnny got there, he saw a heavyset man, seated on a chair and chewing on a cigar. As soon as he walked in, the man stood up and nodded his head. "That's him all right. No mistake about it, Mr. Fitzpatrick."

"I wanted you to be sure."

"But, I—" Johnny looked around in confusion.

"You're a good lad," Mr. Shapiro said. He looked at Fitzpatrick. "The other one, he wanted to rob the car. I was out watering my lawn, like I told you. I heard the whole thing. This lad tried to stop him. Even tried to drag him out of the car. Saw the whole thing."

"You mean—" Johnny stared in disbelief, first at Mr. Shapiro, then at Fitzpatrick.

"That's right," Red said. "You came through with flying colors." He turned to Shapiro. "Thanks a lot, Mr. Shapiro."

"Don't thank me. Thank that lad there for being a good, honest boy. Had enough sense to stop from making a mistake."

A minute later Johnny and Fitzpatrick were alone. Johnny looked up at Red expectantly.

"I told you I had news. I didn't say it was all bad."

"I don't know what to say," Johnny said.

"Well, I wouldn't judge Spider too harshly if I were you," Red said. "His name is Paul Kramer, right? Well, that's the name of the porter who found him in a bus depot. He was an orphan—nobody wanted him."

"But he was living with his aunt, and—"

"Spider didn't have any aunt. Spider didn't have anyone. Not a home of his own—ever. That was a welfare home he was in. And you do."

"I know how lucky I am," Johnny said in a low voice.

"We were coming to get you and Spider yesterday—to settle this thing," Red said. "That's when Ricky and I came driving up, just as you ran out of the park. You remember when the last burglary occurred—at the hardware store?"

"At Terry's dad's."

"Thibedoux's?" Red nodded. "Well, Spider left a print there. And we'd just come from his welfare home—his foster mother had found some money and gum and cigarettes and stuff in the closet. He's on my case list too."

Johnny shook his head. "I can't believe things are coming out this good for me."

"If they are, it's your own doing. You did the

right thing last night. It's a good thing Mr. Shapiro was there. On the basis of what he told me, I'm recommending that no action be taken against you."

"Does that mean—"

Fitzpatrick nodded. "You can go home now, Johnny." He got up to go. "I'll want to see you a little early this Tuesday. Come in about two. We'll have to see the judge—for the record on this." He grinned. "And there's someone waiting to see you."

It was Ricky. He walked in with a lopsided grin. "How you feel, little buddy?"

"Good."

"Good too. You should. You've got a great bunch of pals. They're all proud of you. In fact, Sam and Goggles are out in the car with the folks, waiting."

"Do they know—"

Ricky looked at him for a long moment. "They know all about you, Johnny. You see, last night after that deal happened, when Spider started talking, Fitzpatrick and I had to check out where you were a couple of nights. Just for the record, more or less. And we went and saw some of the guys to verify details."

"Did you tell them—"

"Big deal!" Ricky said. "You think they cared? Ha! Goggles—he was most surprised. You know what he said? He said he didn't see how you could walk around grinning all the time—with all your problems."

Johnny shook his head slowly, a great light dawning on him. "Last night," he said in a low voice, "I—I finally did—did what you told me I should. I just prayed. Honest and simple. I just told God I'd take the first step, and He could worry about all the other steps."

Ricky smiled warmly. "Now you've got it. You know, I have to admit I took a lot longer finding that out than you did. But I was a lot worse at self-pity than you ever were."

"You—"

"I know what it is to be a welfare kid," Ricky said. "You see, Ma and Smiley adopted me when I was eleven. Before that—well, I never knew my father, and my mother ran off when I was a baby, and left me with her sister. And she gave me to the welfare. And, by the time I wound up with Ma and Smiley, I'd been in more jams than you and Spider put together. And I was just wading around in self-pity. But Ma and Smiley laid it out for me in black and white. If I wanted a home and family, all I had to do was reach out and take it."

"But—it sounds so easy," Johnny said. "And it never—"

"It is easy," Ricky said. "And you want to know how I found out?" He stopped and grinned. "I didn't come to preach a sermon, but—well, I can see myself sitting there in you, Johnny. And I want you to find the happiness I found. You said that you'd learned to take the first step? As Smiley told me, it's just like baseball."

"Baseball?"

Ricky nodded. "Let's say you're on first and you want to go to second. Well, you've got to take a lead. Nobody can take a lead for you. And when you take that lead—that first step—you're taking a chance

on getting thrown out. But you've got to take that first step."

"I—I see," Johnny said.

"You took the first step. He'll help you take the rest." Ricky swatted him on the shoulder. "Let's go home, little brother."

Ma and Smiley were in the front seat, while Tom-Tom, Nancy, Sam, and Goggles filled up the back of the wagon.

"Well," Smiley said, pulling away from the curb. "You're ready to come home now, Johnny?"

"You bet!"

"Can I tell him?" Nancy interrupted.

Goggles put a finger to her lips. "Shhh!" He grinned at Johnny. "Boy, if I'd of known. You've got a lot of heart, pal."

"Forget it," Johnny said. He could feel himself blushing.

"He means it," Sam said. "And that goes double for me."

"I wanta tell Johnny!" Nancy broke in.

Johnny looked at her, then at Ma and Ricky. "What's this all about?"

"What day is it?" Smiley said over his shoulder.

Johnny frowned, thinking. "Why—it's—it's my birthday. Today's my thirteenth birthday!"

"Happy birthday!" Tom-Tom shouted. "Happy birthday to you . . . ," he began chanting in a sing-song voice.

"I wanted to tell him," Nancy said, pulling her face down into a pout.

"Well, tell him the rest then, Miss Pouty-face," Ricky said, tousling her hair.

"The rest of what?" Johnny said.

"Well, Sam, and Butch, and Goggly—"

"Goggles!" Goggles cut in. Johnny and Sam laughed and elbowed him.

"Well, anyhow, we're gonna have a party!"

Johnny just stared, first at her, then around the car at Ricky, and Ma, and everyone. "A party?"

"It's your birthday," Smiley said. "And we planned this party a week ago. So—"

"So we've got a party set up in the backyard," Ma said. "Butch and a bunch of the guys are there now."

"I bet they ate all the ice cream up!" Tom-Tom said. "Drive *fast!*"

"You—you mean—you're—" Johnny couldn't think of a thing to say.

Smiley pulled onto their street and a moment later eased into the driveway. Over the fence, Johnny could see the faces of his friends. "Let's go," Sam said.

"And don't eat too much," Goggles echoed. "We can't have a fat man playing third."

Johnny hardly heard him. He sat there for a moment after everyone had gotten out of the car. He was looking off somewhere to where God was— watching.

"Smiley poked his head in the window. "We're home now, son."

Johnny smiled. *Thanks*, he said softly. *Thank you.*

He was home. *Home!*

THE AUTHOR

Dave Hill was born in Minneapolis, Minnesota, and spent much of his youth in the state of Oregon. He has been writing since the age of 24 and has sold stories and articles to most denominational houses. His writings have appeared in *Story Friends*, *War Cry*, *Home Life*, *Hearthstone*, *Words of Cheer*, *Gospel Herald*, *Hi Way*, and other adult Christian magazines.

He is also author of several serials for juniors, *The Big Bible Puzzle Book*, and *Ramon's World*.